Lil Baby
CUFFED BY A
STREET
KING
2

A NOVEL BY

TNESHA SIMS

Royalty Publishing House is now accepting manuscripts from aspiring or experienced urban romance authors!

WHAT MAY PLACE YOU ABOVE THE REST:

Heroes who are the ultimate book bae: strong-willed, maybe a little rough around the edges but willing to risk it all for the woman he loves.

Heroines who are the ultimate match: the girl next door type, not perfect - has her faults but is still a decent person. One who is willing to risk it all for the man she loves.

The rest is up to you! Just be creative, think out of the box, keep it sexy and intriguing!

If you'd like to join the Royal family, send us the first 15K words (60 pages) of your completed manuscript to submissions@royaltypublishinghouse.com

SYNOPSIS

One would think that your enemy would be an unsuspecting close friend; someone who wants to be like you, with you, or even with someone you're with. But, never would anyone have thought that an enemy could be your own parent.

LoVonna was excited to let her parents meet the man she so-called loved. When her father dished out the little he knew about Trigga, Vonna questioned their relationship. When an old lady sitting under a tree spoke knowledge into Vonna's ear, she listened. But it doesn't change the fact that Trigga had a child that she knew nothing about. She gave her heart to Trigga, and he fumbled it. Vonna finds out about her father's past, but it doesn't stop her from wondering why he's the way he is toward Trigga. Vonna is holding a secret of her own, will this secret uncover itself and expose more than she has bargained for?

Trigga knew telling Vonna about his son should have been the first thing he told her when he found out. When Vonna's father brought it up, he knew instantly that he lost her. He knew her father wanted it to happen that way because he didn't want him dating his daughter. Trigga does everything in his power to keep them together. However,

Vonna's father is the least of his worries. Trigga's dad isn't too fond of Vonna. Trigga's father knows what's best for his son, and this new chick isn't it. He'll make it his business to make sure their relationship will end at his doorstep.

Darcel and Larisa's relationship is going great until her father tells her to stop seeing him, or he'll make sure Darcel stays away from his daughter for good. Will Risa take her father as just being overprotective, or will she end things to protect Darcel?

Neen and E are nurturing their relationship back to where it used to be. She doesn't know that soon he'll be nurturing something else that changes their lives forever. Question is, could it be the heart of another woman?

Continue this last ride with the crew in Lil' Baby Cuffed a Street King 2, the Finale.

ACKNOWLEDGMENTS

I just want to thank my Royalty family for their continuous support. I want to thank Porscha for always being supportive and giving me motivation. My Royalty family rocks, and for that, I am honored to be signed with RPH.

To my cousin Terry, I hope you are enjoying my books. I have a lot more coming your way. I love when you call home, and we talk about the characters; that really makes my day. Thank you for your support.

To my sisters, I love you two so much. I appreciate the support and the bond we have. If I can't call on anyone, I know I can call on you two. Maybe you, Kesha, because Terra never answers her phone.

My husband, the one that hears me talk to myself and hears me arguing with my characters and laughing, when you really think that I'm crazy… Thanks for supporting my dream as an author. You know how happy I am when I write.

My wonderful readers, I just can't get enough of the engagement you all give. You ask for more reads, so here they come. Thanks for rocking with me.

PREVIOUSLY IN LIL' BABY CUFFED A STREET KING...

LoVonna

*I*t had been six months since Von and I had been dating. Although it wasn't easy, we were still holding on. I hadn't seen my man in what seemed like in forever, although he did make it a habit of calling when he knew I was out of class and done with my rotation. Jose was standoffish, and I was okay with that. It actually made things easier for me.

"You know Diggy coming later tonight," Risa stated.

"I wish Von was."

"Why don't you go be with him? I'm sure he'll like that. You did tell your mom you were thinking about visiting her."

"Girl, you spoke her up. She's calling now."

Risa got up and left so that I could take my call.

"Hello, Mother."

"Don't *hello Mother* me. I haven't heard, talked, or seen you in like forever," she said to me.

"These rotations and classes keep me busy."

"Is it really classes or is it someone else?"

"What?"

"I met your father in college, remember? I know you are dating someone, so when can I meet him?"

"Mom, you are so crazy."

"You're not good at hiding things, so why don't you come home tomorrow?"

I thought about it, and I did miss my parents.

"Okay, I'll be there tomorrow."

I was actually about to just leave and head there so that I could pop up on my man. I needed to make sure his ass was on the straight and narrow like he'd promised. I told Risa I was about to head out. I packed my things and headed out. On the drive there, Von had called and asked where I was. I told him I was meeting with a friend for drinks, and of course, he didn't like that.

"What am I supposed to do, just stay in the house forever? My rotations have finally ended, and I just want to celebrate."

"I miss you, lil' baby."

"I miss you too. I wish you would have come with Diggy."

"I know, but next week I promise I'll make it happen."

"Okay, but if not, it's cool."

I said that to throw his ass off.

"What the fuck you mean *if not, it's cool?*"

"I meant nothing by it, but I'll call you later okay?'

"Yeah, whatever. You been acting funny."

"How is that?"

"It ain't for nothing, lil' baby. Holla at me."

He hung up, and I laughed. Now his ass saw how I felt when he did the shit to me. I had pulled up to his home three hours later. There was a white Honda in the driveway. I just knew he had a bitch in his crib.

I got out, walked up to the door, and turned the knob. To my surprise, the door was unlocked. I took my shoes off and looked around the house. It was pretty quiet. I walked up the steps, and as I got closer, I heard Von talking.

"Aye, Baby. Don't do that shit again. That's why your ass don't be allowed to come over here, because you don't know how to behave."

I was expecting for a female's voice to say something, but it never came. Instead, he continued to talk.

"You too damn sensitive. Come here, Baby," he said.

I just had to know who he was talking to, so I pushed the door open and walked completely into his room.

"LoVonna?" he asked, shocked.

"Who are you talking to, saying baby and shit?"

"When did you get here? Why didn't you tell me you were coming?"

"I wanted to surprise you. Now can you answer my question?"

"I was talking to Baby. That's my dog's name."

I looked at the dog sitting by his foot. It was a little ol' Yorkie puppy.

"That's Baby, the Pit-bull?"

"I never said she was a pit. You just assumed that shit."

"Wow. All this time, I thought you had a mean old scary dog."

He got up and hugged me. I looked up at him, and we both pulled in for a kiss. It lasted a few minutes before I pulled away.

"Come here, Baby," he said to the dog. As she ran over to him, he picked her up.

"Baby, this is my girl, LoVonna."

I laughed when the dog almost jumped from his hands into mine.

"Aye, she likes you," he pointed out.

"Well is this lil' Ms. LoVonna?" someone asked from behind me. I quickly turned around and saw a beautiful elderly woman. I couldn't help but smile at her.

"Truth, this is my girl, LoVonna. LoVonna, this is my maid, my other mom, my friend, my heartbeat, Truth."

"It's nice to finally meet the woman this boy has been talking about nonstop," she revealed. I blushed, and she came over and hugged me.

Sitting in the living room, we all chatted, and I got to know a lot about Truth as she got to know about me. I really liked her and knew we would become good friends. She left and took Baby with her. I still couldn't believe his big manly ass had that little ass dog. I did overhear

3

before Truth left, that she told Von to 'just tell me.' I wondered what he had to say.

Once he locked up, he walked over to me and stood in front of me. Staring at him, I felt something I never thought I would feel again, especially after Musiq played me. I wanted to tell him. I needed to tell him.

"Why are you staring at me like that?" I asked.

"You are so damn beautiful. I'm so happy you came to see a nigga. You just made a nigga so happy."

"You make me happy," I stated, wrapping my arms around his neck. We kissed, and I felt the shit again. I pulled away and looked into his sexy eyes.

"LaVondrius, I love you."

I said it. I had finally said the L word. He stared at me as if he didn't know what to say. I just knew he didn't feel the same and I immediately wished I hadn't said the shit.

"LoVonna, I love you too, lil' baby."

A smile spread across my face. He picked me up and carried me upstairs as he kissed me. We made it to his room and he stripped me of my clothing. Everything I ever wanted was within him. He was my soulmate, and I was happy to be the one to cuff him.

After showering, I laid on his chest and he played in my hair.

"Remember I snatched your wig off that day in the store?" he joked.

"I'm still not over that, you know?"

We laughed and I just felt butterflies. There was nothing that could break what we had.

"Lil' baby, you cuffed a nigga. I ain't never gave a female all of me. I mean, what Layla and I had was straight at first, but I still did my thing on the side. With you, I can't even think of hurting you."

"Aww, don't make me cry, and I want you to meet my parents."

"Your parents?"

"Yes."

"Aight, when?'

"Tomorrow."

"Damn, you planned this shit?"

"No, I came thinking I was gon' catch your ass up in some shit, to be honest, but now I know you feel what I feel for you."

"You lucky I love your lil' ass, but if you want me to meet them, I will."

"Okay, I'm going to call my mom now and let her know."

"Cool, I have to make a call anyway."

He got up and left the room. I called my mom and held my breath.

"Hey, baby."

"Hey, Mom."

"What up, princess?"

"Well, I want you to meet my boyfriend."

"I knew it. When?"

She was a little too excited.

"Is tomorrow okay?"

"That is fine. Is 4:30 p.m. good? Your father has a showing for a house at 3:30 p.m. He should be done by that time."

"Okay, and I'm nervous for Dad to meet him."

"Why?" she asked.

"I don't know."

"How does he look?"

"Mom, he is so fine."

"Oh, is he? Send me a picture. I don't want any surprises when he gets here."

"I just did, and don't show Dad."

She was quiet, and I was waiting for her response.

"Oh my God. Child, he is fine. How old is he?"

"He's twenty-six."

"Okay... six years apart... not too bad. Well, I'll get my questions lined up for tomorrow."

"Mom."

"I'm only joking, but to hear that you're with someone brings me joy. I hear the happiness in your voice. I'll let you know now that your father will trip about the age thing."

"Dad is eight years older than you."

"I know, but you know your father. I'm happy that you are happy."

"He does make me happy."

"Good, well see you tomorrow."

I ended the call, and I thought about the introductions. I didn't know if telling them I got with him right after he was released from prison was a good idea, but I didn't want to lie because I loved him for him.

It was the next day, and I damn near threw up in Von's ride. He told me to just breathe and relax. Once we pulled up, I noticed my dad wasn't there. I got out, and he jumped out as well.

"What happened to me opening the door for you?" he questioned.

"I'm sorry, baby."

"It's going to be alright."

We walked hand and hand to the door. I opened the door with my key. My mom was in the kitchen, and when she came out, she smiled as if she was watching us at the altar.

"Look at my baby," she told me. We hugged, and I introduced them. She actually told him to call her mom.

"LaVondrius, you are really handsome. I can see why you stole my baby's heart."

"I believe she stole mine first, Mom," he told her.

They were getting along just great, and I couldn't wait for my dad to meet him.

"So, you live around here? How did you two meet?" she asked.

"We met at a party," he told her.

"Vonna's father and I met at a frat party."

"Really? You never told me that," I told her.

"So, what are your plans? I know you have your businesses, but what if Vonna plans to stay where she's living now?" she asked.

"We will make it work. My businesses can take care of themselves, so if I have to follow her, I will."

I couldn't wait to get back to his house so that I could fuck him. He was saying all the right things.

I heard keys, and I knew my father was coming into the house. I looked at my mom and smiled.

"Aye, honey. Whose car sitting out there? It looks like mine."

When my dad saw Von, his expression went sour, and he looked at him with disgust.

"Didn't I see you at the store one day?" he asked Von. I looked at Von to confirm his answer.

"Umm, yeah. I think you did."

"So you're the one who is dating my daughter. What exactly do you do for a living?"

Von had told my father everything he owned and all of his accomplishments. He even told my father about his dad giving him a loan to start his first business.

"That's all fine and dandy, but I don't approve of this relationship. My daughter is twenty years old. She's not ready to take on the responsibility of caring for someone else's child. How does your child's mother feel about her? Have they met? Has she met the child?"

I was confused. What the hell my father was talking about?

"A child? What? Dad, he doesn't have any kids."

"Oh really? So that young boy that was with you that day wasn't calling you Daddy?" my father asked. I looked at Von and the look on his face told me it was true.

"You have a child?" I asked.

"Lo, I can explain. I just recently found out he was mine."

"You have a child?" I asked again, mainly to hear myself say it.

"Joe, you had no right to say all of that. I'm sure he wanted to tell her on his own time."

"No daughter of mine will be playing house with this thug of a man."

"Excuse me, sir, but I'd appreciate if it if you didn't call me a thug."

"I know your kind. You ain't fooling me, son. I see them tats covering your body and the way you walk and talk. You're probably heavy in the streets. Aren't you?"

"Joe, stop it now!" my mom yelled at him.

"No, Tasha. You know you see that shit too. Why would you want your daughter to be with someone like him?"

I walked out the living room and headed out the house. I didn't know where the hell I was going, but being around them had me angry. I was mad at my father for how he treated Trigga, but I was more angry at Trigga for keeping secrets from me.

"Lo, let me just explain," Trigga said, coming after me.

"You lied to me?"

"I didn't lie about anything."

"Vonna, just talk it out. LaVondrius, I am so sorry for the way my husband reacted. I promise we don't judge people, and I'm not judging you. Vonna has always made good choices in life, and I see you being a good one."

"I just need a minute, Mom. Can I use your car?" I asked, being that my car was at Von's house. I knew riding with him wasn't ideal at the moment.

"Sure, baby. I'll get the keys."

"Lo, don't do this right now. Let's just go talk."

"A child? You have a fucking child and you didn't tell me? Even if you did just find out, don't you think that was something I should have known?"

"Yes, and I was gon' tell you, but—"

"But what?"

"Look, I see that you need to calm down, so I'll be waiting when you're ready to talk."

"So just like that, you gon' leave without explaining shit?'

"I'd rather talk when it's just you and I."

He got into his car and sped off. I looked up and saw my mother staring at me.

"You are most certainly my child. I have that same temper."

"Mom, not right now."

"Come take a ride with me," she said.

I wanted to be alone, but I guess I had no choice.

We rode around, and I paid no attention to where she was going.

"You know the reason I'm upset with your father is because he had no room to talk about LaVondrius like that. Your father's past isn't squeaky clean."

"What you mean?" I asked.

"Once you talk with your man, come chat with me again, and I'll tell you everything about your father from when I met him up until now."

I didn't respond. I just looked out the window. I looked up and noticed a crack head on the corner.

"Mom, where in God's name do you have me?"

"The hood, child. This is where your father and I grew up."

"Really? Wow, I would have never thought that, just by looking at the way you two are now."

"That's exactly why you can't judge a book by its cover."

I sat my head back and wondered what message she was trying to give me. My phone vibrated and it was Truth. I had given her my number before she left Von's house."

"Hello?" I answered right away.

"I don't know what happened, but my baby called saying he thinks he lost you."

"I just need some time to get my mind together. I'm sure he told you everything."

"He has, and as a woman, I understand the feelings you are feeling right now."

"Thanks for calling, Truth."

I asked my mother to take me to his house to get my car. I just needed some space from him. Everything was telling me to leave him alone, but my heart didn't agree.

"You didn't say he stayed this far out and look at his home."

"Yeah, my expression was the same as yours. Thanks for bringing me here, Mom."

"How are you getting in?"

"I know his code."

I gave her a kiss, got out the car, and entered the code into the keypad. The gate opened, and I told her I was okay. She backed away, and I headed up the long driveway. I took my keys out of my purse, unlocked the door, and jumped into my car. I headed back toward my condo. I just needed time to think and those three hours were well spent.

9

~

It had been three days since I told Risa about what happened. She was just like my mother, wanting me to let him explain. He called numerous times, but I didn't answer. My mom called and asked if I had talked to him, and I told her that I would soon.

I walked into the park and just took in the people around me. Kids were playing without a care in the world. I saw a few couples walking hand and hand, and men playing with their children, throwing a football around. What stuck out to me the most was an old woman sitting under a tree. She looked up from a book she was reading and fingered for me to come over. I looked around, making sure she was talking to me. When I figured she was, I headed her way.

"Hi. Sorry I was staring at you, I was just taking in my surroundings," I told her.

"It's alright, my dear. Sit."

I sat down. I didn't know why, but seeing her read her bible, I figured she was somewhat of a good person.

"My days left here may not be long. So, I'm going to tell you something that I think you need to hear. If you forgive, a longer and a better life you'll live. Don't go through life holding bad feelings about someone."

I didn't know what to take from that, but I knew God didn't sit her under the tree for nothing. I smiled and thanked her. I got up and walked away cuffing my heart. My mind went to Trigga. *Could I forgive him?* I thought.

To Be Continued...

LAVONDRIUS

"*I* know you're hurting, but sitting around won't bring her back," Truth told me.

"I fucked up. I should have told her the truth, but the truth is, I don't even know if he's my son."

"True, but you can't deny the fact that he looks just like you, Trigga."

"I know, but I have to be sure."

"I understand. I'm going to go call her and see if she'll at least talk to me."

Truth walked away, and I knew Lo would talk to her. She wasn't the type to take shit out on others just because she was mad at someone else.

I called Neen up because I needed her help. She was close to Lo, and I knew she could get her to at least talk to me.

"What's up?" Neen asked when she picked up the phone.

"Sis, I need you."

"Okay, what's wrong?"

"Aight, let me start at the grocery store. I took Volante to the store to get him some ice-cream to bring back to my crib. I come out the store and some OG was parked next to my Roll Royce. He had one similar to mine, but my shit newer. So, we speak and go our separate ways. Before he walks out, Volante calls me 'daddy,' while asking me something. I can't really remember right now. But, anyway, Lo asked me to meet her parents. A nigga feeling her hard so, I'm like yeah. I meet her mom, she was cool as hell. Her pops walk in and say something to his wife about my car outside. Once he sees me, he asked if he saw me at the store. I wasn't gon' lie, so I told him yeah."

"So, her pops was the guy at the store?" she asked.

"Yes, so he asked what I did for a living, and I told him about my business. He didn't seem impressed at all. He just snapped, talking about his daughter was only twenty and wasn't ready to take on the responsibility of caring for someone's child. Shit just went left from there. I tried to explain to her that I just found out, and that I was gon' tell her about Volante. She wasn't trying to hear that. I just left. I didn't want her mom changing her view of me."

"Damn, that's fucked up. Her dad sounds just like Risa's dad. I see why they don't like going around their parents. But on the real, that's hard to deal with. I'm sure she'll talk to you, but you gon' have to really come correct with her, bro. All that shit with Layla, nip it in the bud now. She's not going to want to deal with that drama, I'm telling you."

"I already know, my pops in my ear telling me that Layla is the woman for me. I be ready to knock his ass out."

"When things get back to the way they were, you have to let your father meet Vonna. I don't see how he likes Layla. And I never told you that I saw them out together one day."

"They're always together. I think it's because of Volante, but I don't care as long as she stays away from my ass."

"I'll give Vonna some space and then try to call her and see what's on her mind," she told me.

"Good looking, sis."

"I can't believe lil' baby cuffed you. You and Diggy making history."

"Man, hush all that noise up. I'll hit you later."

I told Truth I was heading to my parent's crib. I wanted to talk to my father because he was pissing me off with all that talk about me being with Layla. I got into my car and headed to his crib. On the way there, all I could think about was Lo. Yeah, it was still early in our relationship, but I was feeling her lil' ass.

"Hey, son, what's wrong with your ass?" my mom asked, once I walked into the house.

"On some real shit, Mother, your husband gettin' on my nerves."

"Oh lord, what is it now?"

"It's Layla. I'm not going to ever be with that chick again. I'm seeing someone else, but with all this shit going on with Volante and Layla, I think I lost her."

"Well, I'll be damned. LaVondrius Truman done fell in love."

I didn't respond because I did have strong feelings for Lo, but the shit with Layla and my father was ruining the shit I was trying to build with her.

"I don't agree with your father about Layla being the one for you. She's nothing like me, so I can't even believe he compared us. However, being that you have a child with her, I think you can be cordial with the girl. What's your girlfriend's name?"

"LoVonna."

"I want to meet her."

"If I can get her to fuck with me again."

"That's different. I never thought I'd hear my son chasing after a woman."

"Not chasing, I just know the shit that went down caused the separation between us. I do love her. I never thought I'd even fuck with a chick on that level again, especially after what Layla did."

"I know I'm not the best mother in the world, but your happiness does mean a lot to me. I know you'll find a way to get her back. So, when you do, I want to meet her."

"I got you."

I went downstairs and found my father on the phone. When he saw me, he quickly hung up and got up.

"That was Layla. She's really hurt that you don't want to work shit out with her."

"Do it look like I give a fuck? I came down here to let you know that I don't want to hear shit else about that bitch. As far as Volante, I want her to get a blood test and fast. Since you talk and hang out with her a lot, give her the message for me."

I blocked the hit I saw coming, but I didn't see the left hand coming at me. He hit me in my jaw. I tried to calm myself down fast, but I guess it wasn't enough to hold me back because I swung on him. He fell and landed on the glass table, shattering it into pieces. My mother ran down asking what was going on.

"What the hell is going on?"

"Your fucking son put his hands on me."

"After you fucking put yours on me. You think because you call yourself my father, I'm supposed to take your abuse? That's all you do is abuse me, more verbally than physically, but that shit stops today. Mom, I'm sorry, but I won't be coming around here no time soon."

"LaVondrius, baby, please, your father just want the best for you, boy. He's trying to make you a legend like him. A man that is feared by all."

"He's not feared by all, so I guess that doesn't make him a legend. I don't fear him, I respected him, but now that shit just went out the window."

I walked away, heading upstairs. I could hear my mother calling me, but I didn't turn back around. I hopped into my ride and headed toward E's crib.

"Hello?"

I answered my phone when Diggy called.

"Yo, bro, Risa just got done talking with Vonna, what the fuck happened?"

I told him everything that went on. He already knew, but I wanted him to know my side of it. I asked did he know where she was and he informed me she was there at the condo. I shook my head.

"Man, this shit is crazy. What? She talking about leaving a nigga?" I asked.

"I mean, she's basically hurt that you didn't tell her bro. I told you to tell her about the lil' nigga."

"But is she talking about leaving me?"

"I think so, look that don't matter because you can make the shit right. Get your girl back. You can't let her cuff you and turn around and let you go. You tap into that pussy, you gon' let another nigga come around and hit what you opened up?"

"Nigga, you already know I will kill over mine. I'm gon' give her some space and come back for mine. Man, I have to tell you about the shit that went on with my father."

I sat on the phone with Diggy as I sat inside my car in front of E and Neen's house. I told him about what happened with my father. He wasn't surprised, he knew the shit would happen one day.

LOVONNA

I was sitting in the living room area with Risa. Diggy went to grab us something to eat because none of us felt like cooking.

"Just call him, Vonna. At least let him explain. I know it's a lot to think about, especially a child. Once he explains himself, you can decide if you want to deal with it or not."

"What would you do?" I asked her.

"I would be pissed, but I would hear him out."

I thought about the old woman under the tree and what she said to me. I had to forgive him, but I couldn't help but feel hurt.

"You should have heard my dad. It was like, he couldn't wait to tell me that Von had a son. My mom has been calling non-stop. I just can't deal with all of that shit right now. I know I wasn't supposed to fall in love with him, but—"

"But what?"

"Nothing, should I call my mom?" I asked.

"Girl, call your momma. I know you're pissed at you dad, but at least talk to her. Hell, I'm still pissed at my dad, but I talk to my mother. She's the one paying my bills. My father wasn't playing when he said he was cutting me off. I just got the new credit card my mom

16

sent me. If it wasn't for her, I would be working a nine to five right now, which I keep saying I want to, but Diggy keeps saying where would that leave time for him."

"Y'all just too cute. That love is rare."

"You can have that with Trigga."

"I doubt that. You think I should call him or do a face to face."

"I would call first, you know his ass high-key crazy."

"Damn, Neen calling. I bet you he's calling from her phone," I communicated to her.

"Go handle that, friend," she told me.

I walked off, quickly answering the phone.

"Hello," I answered as I sat on my bed.

"Hey, boo," Neen said.

"Hey."

"Aww, don't sound so down. Look, Trigga really loves you. Yes, he fucked up, but I think you should just let him explain. He wanted to tell you, but there were some questions about the child being his."

"That's crazy, I feel like I shouldn't even have to put up with no shit like that. A child? How old is the child anyway?"

"He's four years old."

"Are you fucking serious?"

"Just talk to him, he's over here now."

I didn't say anything, I just felt that ache in my heart again. I didn't want to feel hurt over what he did. I wasn't supposed to feel weak for a man, especially him. I didn't even feel that bad when Musiq cheated on me.

"I'll tell Trigga you said it was alright for him to call you, okay?" she asked.

"Yeah, that's fine."

We hung up and I waited patiently for his call. When my phone vibrated, I slowly picked it up, thinking it was him but it was my mom.

"Yes, Mother?"

"Don't 'yes, Mother' me, how you gon' up and leave without telling me?"

"I just needed to get away."

"Running isn't going to solve anything. Part of being an adult means you have to communicate and talk things out."

"I know, Mother."

"Stop saying Mother like that."

"You are my mother, correct?"

"Lil' girl, I will come find you and beat your lil' ass."

I laughed, and she laughed even harder. I could only remember one time when my mother whooped me or cursed at me.

"I'm waiting on him to call me now, so we can talk."

"Over the phone?" she questioned.

"Yes, I'm not there so I can't talk face to face."

"I wanted to talk with you about a few things. When are you coming back this way?"

"I don't know, I'll let you know."

"If not, I'll come to you."

Aw, hell nah! I thought to myself.

"You don't have to come all the way here, I'll let you know when I come."

"Okay, well I love you. I hate things went down the way it did. Trigga seems like a really nice guy and he's handsome."

"More like fine, but whatever."

"Aww, listen to you. Well call me later and let me know how the conversation goes."

"Mom, that's weird to tell you about my relationship problems."

"How come it is? Girl, you better call me! Now that you're grown, we can be friends. I don't have to be tough on you."

She laughed, and I laughed too. I could only remember the million times she told me she wasn't my friend, and that she was my mother. We hung up and I waited for Von's call. I thought maybe he wasn't going to call after all.

I was just about to get up from the bed when my phone vibrated, but it was a FaceTime call. I looked at my phone, and it was Von.

I answered, but I didn't say anything.

"Hey, beautiful," he said. He looked so sexy, and I saw the sadness in his low blazed eyes. I knew he had been smoking.

"Hey, Trigga."

He chuckled, licking his lips.

"I'm Trigga now?"

"What can I help you with?" I asked, ignoring his question.

"Just wanted to see your beautiful face. I know you didn't think I was going to talk to you over the phone. We gon' have to be in-person for all of that."

I just stared at him. I had to go talk to my mom anyway. I just didn't feel like driving all the way back there. It was getting late anyway.

"My mom wants to talk to me, so I might come early tomorrow morning."

"Aight cool, call me when you get here."

"Yep."

"I love you, lil' baby."

"Yep."

"You don't love me no more?"

"Bye, Trigga. See you tomorrow."

I hung up and rolled my eyes. He knew damn well I loved him. Risa knocked on my door and walked into my room.

"You okay?" she asked.

"Yeah, I'm going there tomorrow. Both Von and my mom want to talk to me."

"Talk to you together?"

"Nah, my mom called before he did. I don't know what she wants to talk about though."

"Oh, okay. Well, Darcel is back with the food."

I told her that I would be out in a minute. After eating I came back to my room. I just didn't feel like being in their faces. Diggy was funny as hell, but I didn't want to ruin their happiness by looking down and sad.

◠

It was the next day and I headed to the gas station. It was an early Saturday morning and I was a tad bit tired. Mainly because I hadn't slept all that well. I woke up around five o'clock in the morning so that I could be on the highway by seven, and make it back home to my parents around 10:00 a.m.

"LoVonna?" someone called out from behind me. I was paying for my gas and snacks I bought. I turned around to see my girl.

"Jessica?"

"Hey, girl, how are classes going?" she asked me.

I met Jessica on campus at the school, she was hella smart and crazy at the same time. We talked until she paid for her things and we walked out of the store together.

"I just got a brand-new car," she told me.

"Really? That's good. I was tired of you complaining about your lil' Malibu breaking down every other day."

"Who you telling, but I've been doing these side jobs to get extra money."

"What side jobs?" I questioned her.

"Promise me you won't repeat this."

"I promise."

A part of me didn't want to know. I never knew who was watching or listening close by.

"I do DNA paternity testing. This guy gave me five thousand to do the test on his daughter before he asked the mom for one. Girl, since then, he's been hitting me up to do his other three kids. So, I charged his ass ten thousand for the three. He wants me to do his homeboy's kids as well."

"Girl, are you crazy? Are you doing that at the lab you work at?"

"Yes, only on Saturdays. I'm the only one that works on Saturday. I'm actually headed that way now. I won't get caught. I'm only going to do it enough to stack my account up and that's it. So, if you know someone, let me know. But they have to keep the shit on the low. I don't want nobody telling the wrong people."

"Just be careful, but I have to get going. I have your number, so maybe we can get a drink one of these weekends. You work too damn much though."

"Don't I know it; I wish I had your parents because before I came across this lil' hustle, shit had been hard. The scholarship only pays for so much."

"I get that, but I'll see you later."

I got into my car and pulled off hitting the highway.

LARISA

I was laying across my bed when Darcel came in and laid on top of me. He kissed my neck, and I already knew what he wanted. I had texted my mom and told her that I might come into town.

"Umm," I moaned out loud.

"I love hearing you moan in my ear. That shit turns me the fuck on."

He stripped me of all of my clothing. I sat naked before him as he stared over my body. I watched his eyes as he roamed every inch of me. I turned slowly to give him a better view.

"Damn, I want to suck on that pussy; lay down."

I laid down on the bed, and he pushed my legs all the way back. The way he had me, my foot was touching the headboard. He French kissed the lips of my oozing pussy. I was already creaming because whenever he kissed my neck, it always got my juices flowing.

"Oh my God, you sucking this pussy, baby."

"Umm, I want you to cum on my tongue," he told me. He stiffened his tongue and inserted it inside of me. Once he started sucking, I just let it go. I came on his tongue as he desired.

"You want me to take care of you?" I asked, watching him put his clothes back on.

"Nah, I have to get going, baby."

"I thought you said E could handle it for you," I reminded him.

"He did, but there's other shit I have to handle on my end. Why don't you just come back with me? Vonna there, you can ride back with her tomorrow."

"I didn't want to go back."

"Look, lil' baby, I know you're avoiding your parents. You can't do that. You have to talk to them. I'm not going nowhere."

"I just don't want them to push you away."

"Can't no one push me away from you. Go get packed. I gotta roll."

I quickly packed my things, and we headed out. I texted my mom on the way there to let her know I was coming. She was excited and told me to stop by the house.

It was around 2:30 p.m. when we made it into town. Darcel let me drive his car. He drove his other truck. He had many cars, so it wasn't like he was missing it. I texted Vonna to let her know I was in town as well, but she never texted back.

Walking into my parent's house, I noticed a black truck was parked outside. For some reason, I felt like I had showed up at the wrong time.

"Hey, Mom," I said.

"Hey, doll face." She ran over and hugged me.

"Who's here?" I asked her.

"I'm glad you came by because we really need to talk to you."

I walked further into the living room, and I saw my dad's old friend.

"Hey, Mr. Saliburry."

"Hey, young lady, you have grown up. Larell, she has grown up, man," he told my dad.

"Now you see why I'm doing this."

"Doing what?" I asked.

My mom grabbed my hands and pulled me onto the couch next to them.

"Larisa, I love you with all of my heart. I will not sit back and watch you throw your life away, hanging around this thug. Saliburry, tell her," my dad spoke.

"Tell me what?" I asked. I knew it was going to be something bad.

"Darcel is heavy in the drug game. I'm actually working on a case against him. I'm going to get him, and I guarantee you that he will go to prison for a long time."

"What!" I screamed.

"You heard him right, Larisa. The only way he won't touch Darcel, Diggy, or whatever you call him, is if you stop seeing him."

"Dad, why would you do that?"

I had tears flying down my face. I had to choose whether to let Darcel go to prison or stop seeing him. I looked at my mom, and she just stared at me with sadness in her eyes.

"What is it going to be, dear?" my dad asked.

"Why are you doing this?"

"Larisa, you have a good life ahead of you. I'm not letting some drug lord take you down with him."

"I'll give you a few days to think about it," Saliburry told me. Although I was hurt and confused, I would never send Darcel to prison.

"No, I don't need time. I'll stop seeing him."

My dad smiled, and I walked away. My mom followed me to my old room.

"I'm sorry, Larisa, I'm hurt too. I like Darcel, but I didn't know he was in the streets like that. I can't subject you to that lifestyle. If he was a real man, he wouldn't even want you to be involved in that."

"I'm not involved in anything. I've never seen anything; he's not involved in drugs. How do I know that you and dad aren't lying?"

I was crying, and I felt myself about to snap. I had to calm down because if I didn't, I was gon' take it out on Lanetta. That's my mom name.

"Larisa, we know all about him. Saliburry has been trying to get him for years. If you want to keep him out of prison, just let him go. I don't want to do this, but it's best."

I turned around and walked into my bathroom. I shut the door and just ran colder water over my face as the tears fell from my eyes. I hated them. I knew I could never forgive them for this shit.

I called Neen and had her follow me over to Diggy's house. I parked his car and put his key under the floor mat. I texted him, telling him that it was over between us, and he should just move on. Of course, he called and texted.

My King: Yo what the fuck you mean it's over?

My King: Larisa I'm not playing with yo' ass, you just gon' bail on a nigga like that. We been together 2 fucking years.

My King: You really parked a nigga car at his crib and bailed?

That was the last text I got from him because I had called to change my number. It hurt like hell to let him go, but it would hurt more to see him go down because of me.

"Girl, what the fuck happened?" Neen asked.

"Your uncle."

"What the hell uncle Larell do now?"

"I don't even want to talk about the shit… shit." I started crying again.

"Whatever it is, I'm so sorry. I could only imagine what my uncle said or did. I just hope you realize that you're grown, and you don't have to listen to shit he say."

I couldn't tell her what was going on. It was just too much. I had her drop me back off at my parents' house. I locked myself in my room and texted Vonna. I told her to just let me know when she was ready to leave back to school.

LARELL

I knew I was wrong for what I did, but I wasn't about to let my daughter throw her life away for some thug. Darcel was a smart kid. Yes, he had businesses, but I figured he had some other illegal shit going on as well. That's why I reached out to Saliburry. I found out so much shit talking to him a few days ago.

"What's good, Saliburry?" I asked him. He was helping with traffic as I filmed downtown LA on a new movie. He didn't have to, but he always helped out in the community.

"Damn, Larell I ain't seen nor heard from your ass in a minute. How is it going?"

"It's going, man."

"I see, you got movies coming out back to back."

"Gotta keep the bills paid."

"I hear that."

"Aye, after this let me holla at you about something."

"Aight, I'll be over here when you finish."

Once, I filmed the last set. My crew packed up and left. I walked over to Saliburry. Saliburry was a detective. He was good at his job, so I knew he had all the information on Darcel. We headed to a bar and had a few drinks before I asked him about Darcel.

"What do you know about Darcel?"

"Darcel?" he asked.

"Yes, I looked into this kid, and he has quite a few businesses, but something isn't adding up. His parents are dead and didn't leave him a dime. So, I'm just curious what you got on him."

"Larell, what are you hitting at?"

"He's dating Larisa."

"Baby Risa?" he asked.

"Although she's my baby, she's grown, but I'm not about to sit around and let her throw her life away over him."

"Larell, man, you know how these cases go. I can't just put information out like that."

"What's your price?"

"Really? We're better than that. We're longtime friends. I'll tell you, but that information stays between you, me, and the walls of this bar."

"I got you."

"I work for Darcel."

"Work for? What you mean?"

"I mean, I'm on his payroll. I keep the heat off him, and he breaks me off monthly. Sometimes weekly if I have to do extra work."

"So, what you're basically telling me is that you're not going to mess up your income."

"For the amount he pays me, I can't."

"Well, do me this favor. I want you to—"

My phone vibrated and I had to answer since the crew was going over the edits in the movie. I thought it was my crew, but it was my wife, Lanetta, calling.

"I'm busy right now, honey."

"Larell, Risa said she might come into town. I think she's on her way. I want you to apologize for everything you said to her."

"Honey, I'm on my way home. We have to talk."

I ended the call and continued what I was about to say. Since Risa was on her way, it was perfect timing.

"I need you to scare Risa. Tell her you're going to take Darcel down, and I need you to make it sound believable. Once she's scared, I want

you to hit her with the, 'if she stops seeing him, you'll let Darcel roam free'."

"Damn, you're good. You should do movies?"

"Funny, let's go. You have to tell my wife all of this before Risa gets here."

We headed out, leaving a half drunk beer on the bar top.

LAVONDRIUS

y mom was calling non-stop and Layla was tripping hella hard. My mind was all over the place and a nigga couldn't even think straight. I got up and walked into the kitchen where Truth was at.

"Sit down and eat, boy."

"I'm not hungry."

"I haven't seen you eat today. You said LoVonna is coming, so what are you still tripping for?"

"It ain't even her, it's my damn parents, and Layla and my son keep asking to come over."

"Talk to LoVonna. Once that's over, go get your son."

"You think she gon' stick around?"

"I don't know. I hope she does."

"Well, I'm done here. I'll give you some privacy, don't you start acting crazy on that girl."

"I'm not gon' touch her, you taught me better than that."

"You damn right because that raggedy momma of yours ain't taught you shit but how to roll a damn blunt."

"Truth, chill on mom dukes."

Although she was right, I had no doubt in my mind that my mother didn't love me.

"Whatever, boy, I'm gone."

"You taking Baby with you?" I asked her.

"Nope, I'm going to Bingo. I'll come get her in the morning. Last time I tried to go to bingo with that girl, she cut up."

I chuckled and locked the door behind her. I called Baby and she ran over to me. We sat in the living room, waiting on Lo.

It seemed like hours had gone by, but in reality, it had only been an hour. My phone rang and Baby jumped. I guess we both were waiting in silence.

"Sup?" I asked Lo.

"I'm at the gate," she told me.

"You know the code; come in."

I didn't know why her ass was acting brand new on a nigga. I walked to the door and watched her pull up. It was hot as hell outside. I looked over to my right and noticed a few of my flowers dying. The heat was just too much for them. Truth only came a few days, so I knew I needed to hire a landscaper or gardener to come out daily.

Lo got out and she looked so damn sexy. She wore a half shirt that stopped right before her belly, and she paired it with some capri denim jeans. When she got to the door she stopped.

"Come in," I directed. She was pissing me off acting like she didn't know a nigga.

Closing the door behind her, she took her sandals off. I often told her she didn't need to, but she insisted on doing it. I led her to the couch and just stared at her. I missed her, I missed being in her presence. She sat on the opposite side of the couch. I got up and sat next to her.

"Sit on my lap," I instructed.

"I'm perfectly fine, right here."

"I guess we can jump right into it. Look I just found out that Volante was mine. I swear on everything Lo, I was going to tell you. I just wanted to wait on the right time, and to do a blood test. Honestly, just looking at him I know he's mine."

"Wow, Trigga. I don't even know what to say. A child? How you think I felt when my father blurted that shit out?"

"I know, lil' baby, and my fault about that. I don't know what else to say because it's not like I can put the child back. He's four years old. That bitch could have told me that she was pregnant while I was in prison."

She just stared at me as Baby jumped into her lap. Lo rubbed her, and I faintly smiled.

"She really likes you." Getting closer I felt my heart rate speed of. She had an effect on me that no other woman had.

"I like her too. She's the cutest lil' thing."

"I love you."

She looked at me and smiled.

"Trigga I know it was probably hard for you to tell me, but you should have. Honestly, I can't deal with all of that drama. My main focus is school."

"So, what are you saying? It's over?"

"I just don't think I can deal with all of that. I can't be selfish and want all of your time when I know you have a child."

"That's not being selfish. I want to give you my time, it'll just be divided up."

"I think it's best we let it go."

I didn't say shit. I gave her my heart and she basically tore it into pieces. I wasn't gon' beg her to be with me though.

"I guess I should go. Take care, Trigga."

She got up to walk away, but Baby followed her and jumped around her legs. With an aching heart, I smiled because even my dog wanted her to stay. She picked Baby up and looked at her.

"Aww, I'll miss you too. I'll come over Truth's and visit you."

I watched as she put Baby down, put her sandals on, and then opened the door. She turned around to look at me as if she had something else to say. She never did, she just shut the door and left.

I called Layla and told her to take Volante to my parents and that I would pick him up from there. Of course, she snapped. I hung up and headed to meet them. I took Baby with me because I didn't want to come back home to my shit all fucked up.

Pulling up to my parent's house, I took a deep breath. All I wanted to do was get the child and leave.

"I'm just saying, why I gotta come all the way over here to drop him off? Trigga better stop playing with me," Layla said to my father when I walked into the house.

"First of all, if I say meet me any damn where to get my son, you do that and shut the fuck up!" I snapped.

"Do not disrespect her in my house."

"Nigga, fuck you, you act like you fucking this bitch. I'm so fucking tired of you and this silly ass hoe."

I had to calm down because my son was right there.

"Volante, go get your bag," I told him. He ran off, and I continued on.

"Stop blowing my damn phone up all the fucking time. I told you I was gon' get him. What the fuck you still calling for?"

"Fuck you, Trigga! Ever since that bitch came into the picture, you been acting brand new. I can't stand your ass. I should take my son and move back to Georgia."

"Bitch, please do. I'll pay for the move for you."

"You so fucking cold-hearted. You gon' get yours believe that," she threatened.

"I've heard enough. Trigga, get your son and leave," my pops demanded.

"Get my son and leave? How the fuck you sound, and where the fuck is Ma at?"

"Out spending my damn money. I'll talk to you later because you and I need to have a heart to heart."

I looked at him as Volante came running down the stairs. We left and headed back to my house. I left Baby outside playing in the front, while I went into the house because she wasn't allowed in.

"Let's go, Baby," I told her. She ran over. I opened the door and she hoped in after Volante got into his car seat.

Once at home, I bathed Volante. We watched movies and after he fell asleep, I took him into his room and tucked him in. My phone rang and it was Diggy.

"Yo?" he stated.

"Nigga, do you ever sleep?" I asked him.

"Nigga, sleep is the last thing on a niggas mind. Risa just broke shit off with a nigga."

"Damn, what you do?"

"My nigga, I ain't do shit. I had just sucked the pussy instrumental style. She told me she was going to visit her parents, so I let her drive my car. Hours later, I get a text from her. I'm calling her ass, texting her back and no response. I go to my house and she had my shit parked. I tried calling a few more times, but her ass done changed her number."

"What the fuck?"

"I'm just gon' chill out and see what Neen can find out for me, because a nigga clueless. I just don't know what the fuck happened unless her parents got in her ear."

"That's hella crazy."

"She can't hide from a nigga though. I'm going back when I think she made it back home."

"Man, don't get into no trouble. You paid Saliburry, right?"

"Yep, twenty G's like always."

"Good."

"Well a nigga over here going through it as well, shit. Lo came by, and she thinks it's best we let shit go."

"Shit all bad, but I'm getting mine back. I don't give a damn."

I chuckled because I knew he was dead serious.

ELIJAH

"*I*'m just letting you know to your face that the shit between us is over. I'm not taking it there with you again."

"E, you stay saying that shit, but call me hours later to come fuck me. Why you keep doing this to yourself?" Dasha asked.

"It's over, I can't keep doing my girl like that. I should have never fucked around with you."

I came to Dasha's house to let her know I was ending things between us. Her ass came to the door naked. Although it was hard watching her nipples harden, I managed to say what I had to. Neen meant the world to me, and it was time I made her my wife. I didn't want a fancy wedding, I just wanted her and I to become one.

"Fuck you, nigga. When that bitch pisses you off, don't run your ass over here."

"I won't trust me."

I left and headed to Trigga's crib. My phone rang, and it was Neen.

"Sup, baby?"

"Nigga, you ain't never gon' be shit. All that shit you said to me at my son's grave about being faithful and trying again with having another baby, but then I catch you coming out of that bitch's house! Do me this one favor and go get hit by a fucking bus. I'm so done with

34

you. How dare you talk to my son and tell him you will never hurt me again. You're a fucking liar, E. Don't worry about me. You keep the house, and I'll find somewhere else to go."

After she hung up, I felt like shit. I did tell her a lot of shit at our son's grave and all of it was true. Even if I told her I ended things with Dasha, she wouldn't believe me. I just stared down at my phone thinking if I should call her back when I heard a loud horn. I ran into a truck, and I watched it flip over three times. I stopped and got out to see if they were alive. I knew whoever it was, wasn't.

"My son, someone help me!" a lady yelled. I looked inside the car and she was crammed between the steering wheel and airbag. The little boy looked to be about four years old. He wasn't crying or moving and my worst fear was that I killed him. I dropped my head because if that was the case, I knew I wouldn't be able to look at myself in the mirror.

Inside the hospital, they checked me over. I told them I was fine. I just wanted to know if the boy made it or not. Diggy, E, Neen, and her mom, Justice, came running into the room.

"I'm good, y'all. I just pray that the little boy I hit lives."

"I'm so sorry, E, I shouldn't have said that to you."

I knew what she was talking about, but I wasn't gon' talk about it in front of everybody. I knew she was just pissed at a nigga when she said she wished I'd get hit by a bus. She held me tight, and all I wanted was for her not to leave me.

As we walked out, I heard the doctor call out for the Lopez family. That was the lady I hit. I stopped because I needed to know.

"Your son is doing fine. He's awake, it appears he was just sleeping. I don't know how he slept through the flipping and turning, but it was by the grace of God he didn't incur any injuries. You can go back and see him."

I walked up to the mother while the other family members followed the doctor.

"I am so sorry for what happened. I know my insurance will cover it, but I will also like to give you 200 thousand dollars."

"Sir, it's okay. My son is fine. I just pray you weren't texting while driving."

"Nah, you saw them check my phone. I'm sure they'll pull the records. I just took my eyes off the road for one second."

"That's all it takes. That's why I stopped texting while driving."

I hugged her and turned back to my own family and headed out. Neen and I went to the house. Her mother dropped us off. Neen was on me like a hawk once we walked through the door.

"I'm so sorry, E."

"Baby, it's okay. People say things like that when they're pissed. I just wanted you to listen to me about why I was at her crib. I went to break things off. I told her not to call me and that I wasn't fucking with her like that anymore. I promise you, that was it."

"I believe you."

She hugged and held me tight.

"You're not gon' lose me, baby."

"I pray not, I couldn't take losing you and our son."

"I just want to make love to you. You know I express myself better with love-making."

We entered our bedroom and she took her time taking her clothes off. She seduced me with her eyes. Although I wanted to look down at her body, lil' baby had a nigga eyes locked on hers.

"I know things have been strained between us, but tonight, I'm letting go of all the hurt and pain. I give you all of me. I'm opening up my heart again to you, this time you better cuff it and never let it go. If you hurt me again, I promise on our son I will show you how much I can be a good woman to another man."

I walked over to her because I felt everything she said, but I had to let it be known that she would never make it into the arms of another nigga.

"See, what you fail to realize it that, I will never let that happen. I won't hurt you ever again. But if you ever in your fucking life tell me some shit like that again, I swear yo' ass gon' come up missing."

She licked her lips like her lil' ass was turned on by that. I let her undress me because I wanted her to take control. "It's your world, ma, I'm just living in it."

LOVONNA

I went to my mom's house to talk with her and when I pulled up she was already outside waiting. A smile spread across her face and I couldn't do anything but smile back. She was truly beautiful. I often saw my mother in business attire, but she wore a pair of denim shorts, a fitted t-shirt, and a pair of Michael Kors sandals. Her hair was hanging down with a side part. She looked so much like Valarie Pettiford, it was crazy. It was indeed a hot day but living in California, you kind of just get used to the weather.

"Look at how cute you look. Where you coming from?" she asked me.

"Von's house."

"I see, come in let's talk."

Following my mother around the house, I stopped and asked where my dad was at. She grabbed two bottles of water from the fridge and handed me one.

"Your father is on a business trip; he'll be back Tuesday."

"Wow, that's a long time to be away from you."

"Honey, I be needing a break. Your daddy be wanting it night and day."

"Ughhh! Please don't put those thoughts into my head."

"Oh hush, but tell me what happened with you and LaVondrius."
We walked into the living room and sat down.

"We talked and he explained why he didn't tell me about his child right away, and I told him it's best that we call it quits. School is my main focus."

"God, you're so much like me at that age. Vonna, I'm going to tell you a story. I dated this guy in college. He was so handsome and all the girls wanted him. I was indeed one of those girls. When he approached me, I thought he just wanted one thing. But he started taking me on dates, asking me about my day and classes. I knew it was much more than a sexual thing between us. I started to open up more to him and he did as well. I found out that he was selling drugs to pay for his schooling. Not only that, but he was like a drug lord. He had money and power. Even with me knowing about all of that, I still wanted to be with him. Then out of nowhere, this chick popped up and said she was pregnant by him and boy was I pissed. I broke up with him and didn't talk with him for about two months. I found out that the chick was lying of course, and I beat her ass. Man, I beat her ass real good. Anyway, the guy and I picked up where we left off. He told me that he loved me and that I was all that he wanted. I knew he came from nothing, so that's why he did what he did in the streets, but I helped him get in line to prepare for a better future. By the time we graduated, we were successful. We had invested the money into stocks, CD's, and a few businesses."

"Wait, I thought you met dad in college—when did you meet this guy? And how was y'all together if you were with da—"

I stopped talking when she started shaking her head up and down.

"You're talking about dad?"

"Yes, I am."

"Holly shit! Dad sold drugs?"

"LoVonna!"

"Sorry, but did he? I can't believe this and he treated Von like he was nothing."

So, why is dad going through so much to keep us apart? I asked myself.

38

My mother ended my thought before I could even process what I was thinking.

"Your father knows what it's like to be in the streets. He doesn't want you to get hurt. I gave you the pretty version of our relationship. I dealt with a lot with your father, but in the end, it was all worth it because I loved him."

"But could you deal with a child?"

"I don't know. I can't say unless I was in that situation. I just know you love that boy. I saw it in your eyes and his."

"I'm just speechless right now."

"I knew you would be."

"So, you're telling me all of this so that I could be with Von?"

"I'm telling you all of this, so that you know you can't stop love. If it's true, it will happen. I, nor your father, would be able to come between that. I will say this though, him having a child does bother me, but I can't judge anyone."

"Thanks, Mom. I'm going to bed."

"Oh, you're staying here?" she asked.

"Yes, someone has to protect you while your husband is gone."

She laughed, and I walked away, heading into my old room. I glanced on Facebook and it seemed as if everyone was hurting about something. Someone died, someone got cheated on, or someone got fired from their job. It was depressing. I saw a post from Musiq, and he was at the gym working out. I had to admit, he lost some weight and looked nice. I thought about our relationship, and it was nowhere near the level that Von and I were on.

A text came through from Risa, telling me she had a new number, and asking where I was at. I called her to see what she had going on.

"Bitch, I been calling you all day."

"My bad, I had my phone on do not disturb, but I probably wouldn't have answered anyway with you calling from new numbers and shit."

"Where you at? I need to talk to you."

"At my mom's; come over. It's just me and her."

"I need a ride."

"I'll be there. Shit, we might as well hit Neen up to get a drink."

"Nah, she's getting fucked. It's just you and I."

I laughed but getting fucked was something I wanted. I wanted Trigga's kisses, touches, and licks all over my body. I only called him Trigga when I wanted the dick or if I was mad at him.

Risa and I sat inside of Olive Garden eating. She flirted with the waiter. He was cute, but not cute enough to get killed over.

"I'm not trying to die for you. Diggy gon' kill your ass."

"I broke up with him."

"Bitch! Why?"

Risa told me everything that happened, and a bitch jaw was tired from hanging open at the news. I couldn't believe her dad did that shit to her. I knew I would do the same thing for Von though.

"I'm ready to go back to our condo. I know he's going to come beating the door down."

"You know he is, you just bail on the man without giving him a reason. You think Diggy about to let that shit go?" I asked.

"I already know, but what am I supposed to do? I can't be the reason he goes to prison."

"Did you tell Neen?" I asked.

"No, I called but she was in the middle of fucking."

"Why do people answer if they're getting fucked?" I questioned.

"Shit, hell if I know. I be too focused on a nut to think about a phone."

"Right!"

I usually tell Risa everything, but I chose to not tell her what my mother had told me about my father. Well, at least not at the moment. I just needed time to process my life because shit has been seeming unreal lately. I knew a lot of it had to do with me not doing what I was supposed to. I just couldn't, and I never planned on falling in love with Von.

"My next nigga gon' be a church nigga. Fuck all this extra shit."

"Girl, bye," I said, laughing.

"For real, you know they be the real freaks."

"You mean hoes?"

"Whatever."

"I don't think you're supposed to just get over the lil' break-up this soon. You ain't normal."

"I mean, what I'm gon' do? Just sit around and be pressed about the shit? Hell nah, I gotta get my mind right. These last few classes been kicking my ass," she said.

"Girl, I'm just happy them clinic rotations are done. I have to do my residency, and I don't know where I want to do it at. I guess I might stay in the area we live."

"Yeah, because I ain't coming back here for a while," she stated.

"I understand, but here come your boo."

She quickly turned around thinking it was Diggy, but it was just the waiter. I laughed as she faced me and rolled her eyes.

DARCEL

*I*t's been a few days, and a nigga just been getting by. As a real nigga, you don't just let a bitch come and break your heart. I let Risa cuff me and she bail on a nigga. I don't know what the fuck happened, but I just gave up with trying. I thought about going to her condo, but then I thought about the fact that she changed her number on a nigga. Wasn't no point in me even going after her lil' ass.

My niggas and I had just left from eating out. I was in desperate need of a blunt. Trigga was driving, and he had his seat all the way back.

"Nigga, when you pick that chain up?" I asked Trigga.

"Few days ago. You gotta see my wrist game too, nigga."

"Yo' ass shop like a bitch," E joked.

"Nah, there's a difference. My shit custom-made. You can't just walk into no store and get this shit."

They chuckled, and I just bobbed my head to the music. I thought about the party on Friday and wondered if they were going.

"So, we going to that party Friday?" I asked Trigga and E."

"We is. I don't know about E though, his ass been in the doghouse."

"Fuck you, nigga, I ain't been in no doghouse. Just making my girl happy, but yeah, I'm going."

"You been to your skating rinks, nigga?" I asked Trigga.

"Nah, I need to. Matter of fact, it's ladies' night tonight. I'm gon' roll through and bless 'em with my presence. And it's your rink too. Why the hell you ain't been there?"

"Yeah, let's do that, and shit, I been busy."

In truth, I wasn't thinking about the chicks that would be in there, most of 'em were young anyway. We headed that way, and all I could think about was Risa's ass.

"Damn, it looks different in this bitch," I told Trigga. The manager, Goo, had spoken with Trigga many times while he was in prison. He asked us if he could remodel and change a few things up. Trigga approved, and Goo had that bitch decked out. There was a pool table area where I saw about twelve of them. Another side was a bowling alley and the other side held the skating rink. There was a DJ for each section. It looked more like a club.

"Well, I'll be damned. Mr. Truman done made it out," Goo said.

"Man, I'm liking what you did to the place."

"Had to triple our revenue, man. I'm thinking about doing this to the other one. With y'all blessing of course."

"You got that, I see you got sip and skate for 21 and up now?"

"Hell yeah, it be some fine ass sisters coming up in here."

"Goo, your wife gon' beat your ass."

"She ain't tripping; we did a threesome about a year ago, and she wants to do it again. I think she like getting her pussy suck by a bitch better than me."

"Yo' ass still crazy, man. Let me go see what's all popping in here," Trigga told him. We walked around, and bitches were staring us down. One came over asking Trigga could she apply for a job. We laughed because she didn't give a damn that it was night time. Everyone knew Trigga own the two skating rinks. I wanted to stay behind the scene on things.

E crazy ass put some skates on like he really knew how to skate. That nigga fell before he even made it off the carpet. I laughed so hard, I had to go shit. When I came out the bathroom, a chick was hanging by the men's door.

"Hey."

I looked at her and she was cute as hell.

"Sup?"

"I was watching you from the time you walked in to the time you came to the restroom. I just wanted you to know that you are so sexy."

"Appreciate that, lil' baby, you're a lil' cutie yourself."

"Can we get to know each other?" she asked.

"Yeah, we can do that. I gave her my number, and she did the same. "What's your name?" I asked her.

"Nivea."

"Nivea, that's cute."

"Thanks, what's yours?"

"Diggy."

"Diggy, that fits you."

I looked at her ass and I knew she saw me cock my head to the side. I told her that I would call her. She walked away smiling and I chuckled at how happy I made her.

"Nigga, yo' ass crazy, over there caking and shit," Trigga said.

"Hell yeah, I dropped all my hoes for Risa. I need to recruit."

"Shit, who you telling? I used to have buses of bitches," Trigga stated.

"We done fell the fuck off. I gotta shake this shit," I told him. E looked at us and laughed like he had an inside joke. We spent about another twenty minutes in the rink before we left.

We were chilling at Trigga's house when his father stopped by. He asked Trigga to talk with him in private, but Trigga declined.

"Okay, I just want to apologize for how I been acting lately. I just want you to step up and raise your son the right way. I can't force you to be with Layla. But what I can force is you being back in charge. Diggy, you've done well, but I think Trigga can start back taking over. E, you've always done your job well, and I thank you. Son, I just want you to know I love you, and I'm just trying to prepare you to become a legend like me."

I could see the look in Trigga's eyes, and I just knew he was about to fuck his father up.

"Let me holla at him real quick," Trigga told us.

We got up and gave them some privacy. E called Neen on Face-Time, and I sat beside him waiting for her to come into view. When she did, her ass was naked.

"Damn, baby, you gotta warn a nigga next time," E told her.

"Yeah, don't nobody wanna see that shit," I told them. I had gotten up and went to the other couch. I didn't look at Neen like that; she was like a real sister to me. She apologized to the both of us. I drowned them out and glanced at my phone. I wanted to call Risa but didn't have her new number, and I wasn't going to ask Neen for it. I did wonder what she knew about Risa breaking up with me.

"Aye, ask sis why her girl do me like that?"

"Baby, Diggy asked why Risa dump his sorry ass?"

"He didn't say it like that; I can hear him. Tell Diggy I didn't even know they broke up."

After that, I got up and grabbed the phone. I told her everything. She hung up with us because she wanted to call her.

LARISA

*A*lthough I was missing Darcel, my main focus was on school. My grades were all A's and I felt good about it. I had just left my last class, and I decided I wanted to just hang out and have a little fun. I no longer had classes on Thursday, so that freed up my Thursday and Friday's. Neen had called a few times, but I had yet to call her back. I decided it was a good time to call her while walking to my car. I noticed my reflection in my windows, and I just stared at my appearance. I wore a blouse and a pencil skirt with a pair of Steven Madden heels. My mom always said to dress to impress wherever you go.

"Because you are my cousin; I'm not going to snap on your lil' ass."

"I'm so sorry, Neen. I just been trying to focus in school. Every time I tried or thought about calling you back, something just came up. Plus, I'm starting my internship soon, so I been busy getting things in order for that."

"Yeah, that better be it, but what the hell happened between you and Diggy?"

"Long story. I rather tell you in person but being that I'm not coming there no time soon, I guess the phone will have to work."

"Yes, don't make me come there because then, it'll be a problem."

"Shut up, but anyway, I went to visit your uncle and aunt one day, and they had company. It was one of my dad's friend. But not just any ole friend. It was Saliburry, a DEA agent. He's a good friend of my dad's, and he told me that he's working on a case against Darcel. He told me that if I stopped seeing Darcel that he would not take him to prison. You already know my dad had a lot of shit to say as well?"

"I'm going to come there tomorrow. We need to talk. But first, I need to talk to the crew about some shit. I love you cousin, and I know that your dad just wants to protect you, but he is really fucking wrong for doing that shit. I work tomorrow, so I need to make sure my assistant can cover everything before I leave."

She hung up, and I just stared at the phone in shock. I didn't know why she thought she needed to come see me, but I knew she would only try to talk me into staying with Darcel. But to protect him, I can't be with him.

I pulled up to the condo, and Vonna was walking into the house. I called out to her. She turned around and smiled.

"I got your text, hoe. I see you got all A's. I knew you would. I got all A's too!"

"Bitch, that ain't nothing new. Your ass always gets A's," I reminded her.

We walked into the house and I told her the conversation I had with Neen. She said Neen was probably just coming to check on me. Neither of us felt like cooking, so we ordered a pizza.

"Let me tell you what happened to me today. So, Jose and I was talking, just having a normal conversation, and he asks if I was still seeing Von. I told him yeah because I don't want him to start coming on to me, because the way this kitty feeling down here, I might just call the nigga to just come hit it. I know if I do that, Jose ass will go crazy. He's like the clingy type."

"Yo' ass crazy, but I know the feeling. This shit hurts so bad because the one nigga I want to hit it isn't allowed to be around me. You know how Jay-Z said, 'catch a charge, I might' in the song with Beyoncé? Well, if Darcel hit this pussy one more time, he's definitely going to catch a charge."

"Girl!" Vonna laughed so hard, but I was dead serious.

"Vonna, I'm serious, man. I keep thinking about just letting him hit it every now and then. We ain't gotta be together."

"You are really crazy. Don't no normal female say shit like that."

Vonna went to shower and as soon as she walked off, the doorbell rang. It was the pizza. We already paid online. So, I just signed the receipt and shut the door. I went into the kitchen and placed the pizza and wings onto the island. I washed my hands and took two paper plates out for us.

Vonna finally came out with shorts and a tank on. I could clearly see that she didn't have any panties or a bra on.

"Your ass always naked."

"I have clothes on."

"Barely."

"Oh, my girl Jessica invited us to a party she's having tomorrow, you wanna go?" she asked me.

"Yeah, we can do that. I might meet someone I like."

"Diggy gone fuck you up."

"I'm not with him, so."

"You think that."

"Whatever, there isn't shit I can do. When it comes to Larell, he always wins."

"I can't believe your dad. At least my father's main concern was that Von had a baby, but then again, he thought he was in the streets as well. Shit, I really don't know why he doesn't like Von."

"They just want to ruin our lives, that's all."

"I have to tell you something. Promise me you won't repeat it and especially not to your parents."

"Do it look like I tell them anything?"

"You're right, but remember that evening you called me, you had just changed your number?"

"Yeah."

"My mom told me that my dad used to be a drug lord. He was deep in the streets, but he got out."

"Shut the fuck up."

"I swear to God."

She went on and told me everything her mom told her about her father. I couldn't believe the shit. It was crazy if you asked me because he wasn't one to be judging Trigga.

"I can't believe our fathers. I wonder if my father was in the streets."

"Who knows? The way they act you, wouldn't know."

It was getting late, so we headed to our rooms. I showered and played with myself until I came. It wasn't the same because I wanted something pounding against my pussy. I almost got the hairbrush to use the end of it, but I knew that shit was nasty and could possibly fuck me up. I was just too damn horny. I walked to Vonna's room to complain.

"I'm horny as fuck!" I shouted after bursting through her door.

"Bitch, and why you come in here to tell me like I can help you? You better take a cold shower."

"I hate you."

"I love you too," she said as I shut the door.

It was Friday, and it was time to go out. I was happy because I just wanted to get my mind off all the bad things. I wore a two-piece outfit that was made up of a white spaghetti strap top and coral bodycon long pant with a belt. I curled my hair after having my Brazilian straight hair installed. Vonna wore a wine colored cold shoulder tunic top swing t-shirt dress, that also had pockets.

"Does this bun look okay?" Vonna asked me.

"Girl, yes, that style always looks good on you. And it shows off your pretty face," I told her.

There was a knock at the door and I looked at Vonna.

"What if that's Darcel?"

"We will find out, won't we?"

She strolled over to the door and peeped into the peep hole. It was Neen.

"I forgot you were coming. Why didn't you call to remind me?"

"Had to take care of some shit today and I didn't know I had to remind you that your favorite cousin was coming."

She looked us over. I knew she approved of our outfits.

"Y'all look cute, but where y'all going?" she interrogated.

"To a party; you wanna roll?"

"Nah, I need to talk to you about some real shit. After I tell you this, you ain't even gonna wanna go out."

I didn't know what to think. *Was it Darcel? Was he okay?*

"Just tell me because my mind is already whirling."

She walked over to the couch and sat down. I guess that meant I needed to take a seat as well. Vonna sat down next to me.

"Remember you mentioned Saliburry on the phone to me?" she asked.

"Yeah, what about him?"

"Saliburry is on payroll for Trigga and his whole crew. He keeps the cops and anyone else with authority in the jurisdiction system off them."

"Wait, what? Why would he tell me out of his own mouth that he will take Darcel to prison?"

"Because like you said, he's your father's friend. He just did him a favor and lied."

"I can't believe this shit. How do you know all of that?" I asked.

"Because they had a meeting and Diggy asked Saliburry why the fuck he tell you some shit like that. It took all of them to get him off of Saliburry."

"What the fuck? This can't be real. What did Saliburry say?"

"What I told you, he did it for a friend."

"You mean to fucking tell me that I went without dick for that long over some fucking bull shit? My father is really acting like my damn enemy instead of a fucking father."

"He was dead wrong for that shit, but you better go get your man," she told me.

"I feel like shit, I should have been told you about this shit. Now look. He probably doesn't even want to talk to me anymore."

50

"Yeah, but he's just pissed. You know how niggas get. He felt like you should had come to him about the shit, but that don't matter. We have to get on the highway so you can go get your man."

I looked at Vonna, who was quiet the whole time.

"You okay with not going out?" I asked her.

"Girl, go get your man."

"You're coming too, right?"

"I can't. Remember I have that important meeting about my residency tomorrow? Saturday was the only day we could meet because our schedules didn't align with one another."

"Shit, I forgot, well we can wait until morning because I don't want to go without you."

"Boo, you don't need me. And besides, you could be getting fucked late into the night if you leave now. You need to, how horny your ass was last night."

"Shut up, but I'll wait for you," I told her after laughing.

"Good, because I'm tired anyway," Neen told us.

Vonna and I changed out of our clothing and just chilled. Neen had went back to her car to get her bag and also brought some wine.

LOVONNA

$\mathscr{I}$ had just finished my meeting about my residency.
Everything went well, I just needed to make my mind up
about where I was going to do it. As I drove off, I thought about Risa.
Her father was so out of line for doing what he did. I was happy Neen
told her everything, because I knew how much Risa loved her some
Diggy no matter what.

Heading home, I thought about the lady under the tree. For some
reason, I wanted to know if she would be there. Instead of turning on
the next street to get to my condo, I kept straight, driving toward
the park.

I got out and looked around, but I didn't see her. I saw someone
cutting the grass, so I thought I'd asked to see if he knew where she
would be.

"Hello, sir, have you ever seen or noticed an older lady sitting
under this tree?" I asked him. He turned the lawn mower off and got
closer. He asked me to repeat what I had asked, and so I did. He was a
white male who looked to be about thirty-something.

"Oh, yes, Mrs. Coria goes to the church about ten minutes
from here."

He pulled his phone out of his pocket and gave me the exact address.

"If you go now, you will catch her before she leaves. She goes every Saturday morning for the little kid's morning activities."

"Thank you, sir."

I quickly walked away because I wanted to catch her before she left like he told me.

Pulling up to the church. I got out and walked in. I was greeted by a younger girl, and I asked for Mrs. Coria. She had me take a seat while she went to go get her. About two minutes later, she walked in and smiled.

"Hi, Mrs. Coria, I'm LoVonna. I don't know if you remember me, but I met you under that tree at the park. Remember, you called me over?"

"I know who you are, beautiful. What can I help you with?"

"I just, umm… I just wanted to talk with you."

"Of course, come walk me outside. I do have to get going, but I can spare a minute for God's child."

I didn't know why she called me 'God's child', but I took it for what it was. I looked at her and even though she was an elder, she looked good for her age. She wore a black blouse and ivy slacks. I glanced down at my attire. I was happy I had went to a meeting because my attire was appropriate for the church house.

"So, what do you want to talk about?" she asked once we got outside.

"Well, I'll be brief so that you can get going. You had said something about forgiving. Well this guy I was dating withheld some information from me because he felt it wasn't the right time to tell me. I found out through someone else, however, the situation is more than I had bargained for. So, I broke up with him."

"I know I said I only have a minute, but I need you to be more detailed than that," she stated.

"He has a son that's four years old. He just found out about him."

"I see. Well, how old is this guy?"

"He's twenty-six, and I'm twenty. I'm a college student, and I took a lot of classes to get ahead. I'm in my second year of school to become a physician, and I'm already at the point to start my residency."

"Oh, so, you're in medical school? Honey, I will tell you this. Love doesn't have a filter. There are going to be things that you'll have to accept and somethings you can compromise or substitute from, but you won't be able to get rid of it. If you love him, like I'm sure you do because you went through all of this trouble to come find me. But if you love him like you do, his son wouldn't be an issue. Are you pushing him away for another reason?"

I thought about her question for a minute. I knew she had to leave, so I gave her the honest truth.

"Yes, my father doesn't approve of our relationship. Although I made it known that I didn't care about what my father thinks, I really do."

I hated the fact that I had to lie in church, but I couldn't say what I was really feeling.

"You can't please others when it comes to matters of the heart. You can only fulfill what matters most to you."

"You're so right. I'm sorry I kept you longer. I really appreciate your advice. That's why I came looking for you. I asked the guy cutting the grass in the park if he had known you, and he directed me here."

"It's quite alright, young lady. I just hope you deal with what's in your heart and not what anyone else has to say."

"I will."

Once we finished. She hugged me and gave me her number. I gave her mines too. I looked at the clock and knew I had to get home so we could hit the highway.

When I got home, I didn't think about the fact that I would have to drive because we needed a way back. I wanted to sleep the entire drive there, but that wasn't happening. I changed my clothes to something more comfortable. I placed on some black legging shorts and a crop top that read *Miss Me*. I listened to my girl Monica all the way there.

We pulled up to Neen's house, and she let Risa drive one of their cars to go see Diggy. Neen asked where I was going, and I told her I'd probably go see my mom.

I was pulling out of Neen's driveway when I decided to call Truth.

"Well, I thought you dumped me too."

"No, it was never like that. I'm here in town, I umm… I was just checking to see how you were doing."

"I'm fine, but I know why you really called. He's okay, but he misses you. All he talks about is how his lil' baby does this and how his lil' baby does that."

I laughed, but it felt good to know he missed me.

"Where are you now?" I asked her.

"At his house. I just finished cleaning. He's not here. Why don't you stop by?"

"I don't know if that's a good idea, especially with him not being there."

"Child, bring your tail on. He won't be back for a while."

"Okay, I'm on my way."

I sat at Von's gate thinking if I should really go in or not. I knew Truth would be mad if I didn't, so I put in the code and headed in. Driving up, I thought about Von. My love for him was true, especially when Mrs. Coria told me those things. I knew I had to reach out to him because I was wrong on so many levels to do him the way I did.

After parking and sitting for what seemed like forever, I finally got out. When I walked up to the door, it came open and Truth stood before me with Baby. Baby barked and ran to me, and I started to laugh.

"Come in," Truth stated.

We sat on the couch talking about what I been through with schooling and of course my feelings for Von. We were just finishing up talking about him when he called her. I rubbed Baby, and she sat on my lap as if she was asleep.

"Yes, sir," Truth responded to him as she put the phone on speaker.

"Don't call me that, but I'm like ten minutes away, you need anything?" he asked her.

"No, I don't, do you need anything besides groceries?" she asked.

"Nah, I'm good. When are you going to the grocery store?" he asked.

"Now, in fact I'll be gon' by the time you get here."

"Aight, take Baby with you because I'm stepping out tonight. I might bring me a little freak back to the crib."

"You will never do that, you have never brought a girl back to your home besides LoVonna," Truth stated, winking at me. I couldn't wait to hear his response.

"You're right, but look where that got me."

She looked at me, and I stared back at her. I felt bad, but he had to understand how I felt.

"We'll, I'm leaving. I'll be back later with your groceries."

They ended the call, and she gathered her things up to leave.

"Well, when he sees your car out there, he'll be surprised."

"No, because you're going to drive it to the store. He won't even know I'm in here until he gets in," I told her.

"I like your thinking."

Once her and Baby were gon', I made my way up to his room to inspect. I heard what he said about bringing a freak back to his crib. I looked around but didn't see anything that told me a female has been there. I still had my sandals on because I didn't want him to see them by the door. I took them off and placed them beneath the bed. I laid in his big ass bed because for one, it was so soft, and two, I missed laying in it.

I heard him come in, and he was on the phone. He was yelling at someone, but I wondered who. I got nervous when I heard him get closer, then I heart a clink sound. Almost like a cocking of a gun. Von entered the room with his gun pointed at me. Once, he saw that it was me he put it away.

Von stood by the door as I laid on his bed looking over at him. We stared at one another until he spoke. He must have thought I was an intruder.

"You break shit off with a nigga after I let yo lil' ass cuff me. Now you're lying in my bed. You're lucky I didn't shoot first."

"I'm sorry, Trigga. I was wrong to do you like that. I can't deny that

I love you, I want you, and everything that comes with you, and I want it."

He walked over to the where I was and stood on the side of the bed. I hated that he just stared at me and didn't say shit. I got up on my knees and went to him.

"I'm so sorry Trigga."

"First, stop calling me that, that ain't what you call me. Second, why now?"

"What you mean why now?" I asked him.

"Why do you want me now?"

"I never stop wanting you. I love you, LaVondrius."

I placed my hands on his waist and peered up into his eyes. I missed those eyes. Those tattoos were calling for me to kiss on them.

"How you get here?" he asked.

"I drove, Truth is in my car, and I wanted to surprise you."

It was silent for a moment, and he looked down at my chest.

"I do, lil' baby," he told me.

"You do what?"

"Your shirt says miss me, and I do miss you."

"Aww, baby, give me a kiss."

He kissed me, and it felt just like the first time we kissed. I started sucking on his tongue which I knew always made him want it. I wanted it too and so, I went for it. I unbuckled his belt on his designer shorts. He pulled them down, along with his boxers. He stepped out of them and stroked his dick with his hand.

"He misses you," he told me.

Von was big as hell, but I wanted to please him, so I had him lay on the bed while I sucked on his 'snake' as he called it.

"Damn, I miss you, baby."

I was sucking like it was the last dick I'll ever suck again, which it was because I would never pleasure another dude as I pleasured him. I just couldn't wait for him to return the favor and dick me down properly.

DARCEL

I walked to my door because someone was ringing the doorbell like crazy. I was surprised I didn't hear my damn dog barking. When I opened the door, I knew why he wasn't barking and it was because Risa stood on the other side of it. My dog loved that girl as I did.

"What the fuck do you want?"

"Darcel, please don't be that way. I only agreed because I thought it would keep you out of prison."

"You just up and leave a nigga without even talking to me. We been together for two fucking years and you pull that shit."

She stepped in and shut the door behind her. She placed her hand on my heart and looked into my eyes.

"I'm sorry I hurt your heart, it was never my intentions to hurt you, baby, I swear. I wanted to protect you. I didn't know my father would go through that much to keep us apart."

"You making a nigga feel soft as fuck," I told her.

"I don't care about all of that. I just want your heart back. Please tell me it's still mine."

I looked at her and smiled. She had on a purple shirt and pair of white shorts. Her white wedge shoes complemented her legs. I wanted her legs wrapped around me while I fucked her to sleep like I always did.

"You still got a niggas heart cuffed, lil' baby, don't worry."

"Aww, I love you so much."

"You lucky a nigga was about to get ready and move on with another chick. I would have had her on my arms loving a nigga hard," I told her.

"Don't play with me, I'll fuck around and have your ass crying with a new nigga carrying me in his arms. Don't start no shit, it won't be no shit."

I had to remind him who the fuck I was.

"Yo, that shit ain't funny. You act like a nigga, what I tell you about that shit? Be soft around me."

"Shut up and come fuck me. I've been so horny."

"My pussy been tampered with?" he asked.

"Never, it's ready for its rightful owner."

"Yes, it is, lil' baby, you're already dripping wet for a nigga. Come sit on my face first. I want to taste those juices." He already had his hands inside of my shorts.

I laid down and Risa positioned herself onto my face so I could suck on her pussy. I stared into her eyes while I kissed, sucked, and licked her spot. Her shit tasted so good. I didn't make a habit of eating pussy in the past, but Risa had me wanting to eat her all the time. I raised her up and slipped a finger into her ass. She started moaning even louder as I continued to suck on her.

"Damn, Darcel, you making me come. I can't hold it."

"Let it go ma, come all over my face baby."

Risa came long and hard. It was my turn to enjoy the feeling of her pussy instead of my tongue.

After making love to her until the evening, I finally let her lil' ass go to sleep. I woke her up and asked her about the shit her father pulled.

"I don't know what his problem is. I can't... umm, my pussy jumping. You always do this to me."

"Girl, finish with whatever you were about to say."

"I was just saying I can't believe he would do something like that. You're an awesome man and if he can't see that, that's his problem. Thing is, he acts like he's perfect but he's far from perfect."

"I just don't want you going against your father for me, lil' baby."

"Darcel, I will go to war for you, especially for that dick. That's what I missed the most."

"I bet your ass serious too."

I laughed at her crazy ass. I knew she didn't want anymore because her ass was drifting off to sleep. As always, she couldn't take a good dick slaying.

LAVONDRIUS

*I*t was early morning and the sun was shining through my curtains. I made love to Lo all night. She expressed her feelings for me, and I did the same. I told her more about my son. I also told her that I was just started to get to know him more, so I wasn't ready for her to meet him just yet. I wanted her to meet my parents though. The night my dad and I had that long talk, he kept saying he wanted to meet Lo. But I didn't tell him that we were officially over.

"Awh, fuck!" I said out loud to myself. I had told Layla I would meet her and my son at the mall to buy him some more shoes and clothes. Lo was still in the bed and I had taken a shower and got dressed before coming into the kitchen for something to eat. Truth must have had come in and put things away and left. Lo's keys were on the counter, so I knew her car was outside.

I finished my cereal when Lo had just walked in. I called her over and told her about Layla and Volante.

"Well go, you said you're going to buy him shoes and clothes. I'm sure he's looking forward to it."

"I just don't want you to think I'm putting you second."

"Even if it was you putting me second I wouldn't trip. He's your son, so I have to respect that."

"I still need a blood test."

I showed her his picture, and she said he was mine. It was crazy because he looked so much like me too.

I left Lo at my crib and met Layla at the mall. She thought it was family day, but I had to remind her ass why we came to the mall in the first place.

"Trigga, you don't have to be mean, at least let my son know you care about his mother," she indicated.

"That would be lying to him because I don't care about your ass."

I just bought him four pairs of shoes. I already had Neen bag his stuff up that my designers made. We walked out the mall, and I walked them to her car. It wouldn't start, and I could tell it was the starter. I called for someone to tow it to the shop. I didn't want her ass in my car, but I knew I was being petty about the shit.

I took Volante to get something to eat. Layla tried her best to make small talk with me, but I wasn't having that. We were there for our son only. I texted Lo and told her I missed her. She sent all types of emojis back.

"Who the fuck got you smiling so hard, you about to run us off the road from looking at that damn phone."

"I pray someone run your ass off the road, and don't worry about who got me smiling. It ain't yo' crazy ass."

"How did we get to this point, Trigga? I still love you."

"How about when you left a nigga hanging when I got knocked. That's how we got to this point. And you say you still love me, well that's too bad because I don't love you."

"I already told you I was scared because I found out I was pregnant."

"I'm seeing someone else, and soon I'm going to let Volante meet her, but first I want a blood test."

"So, is this bitch telling you to get a blood test done on our son?"

"You sound dumb, and she just found out about him. I asked about that shit a long time ago, and she ain't even like that. My son isn't her concern he's mine."

"I'm not feeling any strangers around my son, so I'm going to say no."

"You can't say shit if I want to have my son meet my woman that's what's gon' happen. Let me hurry up and get this boy something to eat so you can get the fuck out of my car."

"You're so fucking disrespectful. Don't make me hate you. I'm trying not to be that baby mama, but you're making it hard."

I looked at the bitch like she was crazy. I admit she did have a right to say who was around our son. But Lo and I were official. She cuffed a nigga and shit was solid between us.

"You're worried about the wrong fucking thing. Check yo' fucking self and get it through your head that we are done."

She shook her head and pulled her phone out. Now her ass was texting someone. She didn't have any friends, so I knew it was either my father or mother.

Once I dropped them off, I went back home to Lo. She was smiling when I got in and that shit made my day. Being around Layla had a nigga frustrated as hell. I told Lo what happened, and she said I needed to have a good relationship with Layla for Volante.

"Baby, you don't know this chick like I do. She's crazy as fuck, and I know she's going to use him to get to me. I can already see the shit now."

I followed her back into the kitchen. She sat down and ate.

"Just be nice, Von. You don't have to disrespect her to get your point across. You are the one that laid down with her in the first place."

"You're right, maybe I can be a lil' nice. But she'll take that as me wanting to be with her ass."

"Oh, hell nah, I guess you can be mean to the bitch then," She told me with a smile.

I looked at her and shook my head while she ate her food.

"But for real, you should be cordial with her for your son's sake."

"I'll try, lil' baby. So I know your father don't like me, but I want you to meet my parents."

"What?"

I glanced at her funny when she blurted it out like that.

"What you mean what?"

"I umm… I just meant when?"

"Tomorrow possibly, but I'll check."

"I'm already nervous."

"They'll love you, baby."

"How do you know that?"

I didn't know, but I was praying that they did.

LOVONNA

*V*on and I came to my mom's crib so that I could change because I had left my things at her place, but I also wanted her to talk with him again while my dad was gone.

They chatted downstairs while I got dressed. I could hear them talking about me while I changed. After I finished we were headed over his parents' house.

"She always has to throw all the trash away out her room before she goes to sleep. I just be wanting to tell her to just lay down," Von told my mom.

"Oh my God, she has been doing that since she was little. I think she has some OCD issues. Have you noticed that she doesn't use the same dry towel more than once? I used to get so mad when washing clothes. I had to tell her to at least dry off twice with it before she threw it in the laundry basket, but it never happened, she thinks that is so disgusting."

"You know I have, but I never said anything, but now that you have mentioned it, she does do that."

"Why are you guys talking about me as if I'm not here?"

"You look beautiful," they both said, looking over at me.

"Are you guys sure? I don't want to send them the wrong message with my attire."

"LoVonna, you are trying too hard. If they don't like you for who you are, then that's their problem. No offense, LaVondrius," my mother stated.

"None taken, and I keep telling her to chill because they will love her."

We left and headed over to his parents' home.

I kept looking at myself in Von's mirror. I don't know why, but I really wanted them to like me. I guess since my father didn't like Von I thought that if his parents didn't like me, it would ruin our relationship. I wore a nice rose color blouse with a pair of skinny jeans and royal blue heels that went with my royal blue purse.

"We're here," Von announced. I looked up in awe.

"This is a fucking mansion. Your house ain't shit compared to this."

"Well thanks," he told me.

"Sorry, I'm just nervous, Von. Maybe we should reschedule this meet and greet shit."

"LoVonna calm yo lil' ass down. It ain't even that serious. Their just regular people. Stop acting like they're the president and first lady or something."

"The way this mansion looks they could be."

"Come on, lil' baby. Yo' ass is crazy."

We got out and he grabbed onto my hands.

"Sweaty ass palms, calm down, baby. Just relax, just be yourself okay?"

He kissed me and peered into my eyes. I smiled and tried my best to relax as much as I could.

We walked up the stairs to their home. I felt like there were a million of them. He walked into the house and announced that he was there. Everything was so spacious and big. I looked to the ceiling and it was so high up. One side was all glass.

I heard footsteps and then a woman's voice coming closer to us. I must have been really nervous because we were actually walking toward her into a living room.

"Mom dukes, what's up!" Von yelled out as she walked from another area.

"Awe, is this LoVonna? She is gorgeous, boy. I see why yo' ass so sprung. Girl, you got my son nose wide open!"

I didn't know what to think of her loud ass talking; she was yelling when we were only a few feet away.

"Yes, let me introduce y'all first, damn, Ma. LoVonna this my mom, Tanah. Mom, this is LoVonna."

I extended my hand, and she shook it. I don't know why I thought she was one of those moms who would look at my hand and dismiss it to pull me in for a hug.

"You can call me Vonna," I told her.

"Okay, Vonna, well dinner will be ready soon. Trigga, your father is downstairs. Go get him."

Trigga walked off, and I was nervous to be left alone with his mom for some reason.

"Vonna, can you cook?" she asked.

"Yes, I can."

"Okay, well come help me in the kitchen. I already did the major stuff, I just need a few more things done."

Following her into the kitchen, I just was amazed at everything. The stove was in the middle of the island and it was big as hell.

"You have a lovely home," I told her. She told me to have a seat at the stool.

"Appreciate that. Vonna, do you have any kids?" she asked me.

"No, I don't."

"How old are you?"

"I'm twenty."

"Here, you can cut up these carrots and potatoes," she told me. I took the utensil that she gave me and went to work.

"What is it that you're doing? Are you in school, working, what?" she asked.

"I'm in school to become a physician."

"Wow, that's great. How much longer do you have?"

"I'm in my second year. I have two years left of college, but the

67

residency program is a little longer before I can practice on my own. I want my own private office."

"That's impressive, so are you aware that Trigga has a child?"

"Yes, Von told me he has a son."

"Von? I never heard anyone call him that."

"Yeah, I don't like to call him Trigga."

Unless I'm mad or he's hitting my spot, I thought to myself.

"Are your parents still living?"

"Yes, they are."

"And what do they do?"

"My mom is a defense attorney, and my dad owns his own real estate."

"Wow, silver spoon. I know you had it easy."

I couldn't believe she said that. Yes, my parents took good care of me and set me up to succeed in life, but I wasn't one that was shy of hard work.

"Well, I wouldn't say that. I'm a hard worker and I'm humbled."

"Yes, you are. Do you think you will marry my son?" she asked.

I didn't know how to answer that.

I was happy when Von and an elder man who I assumed was his father walked into the room, because Von looked exactly like him.

"LoVonna. this is my father, Volante. Father, this is my girl LoVonna."

"Nice to meet you," I said to him. I was sitting at the island cutting the carrot. I went to shake his hand and he stared at it for a brief moment."

"I didn't wash my hands and I see you're helping my wife, so I'll have to decline your gesture," he told me. I felt like he didn't like me off rip, but I put those thoughts away. I went back to finish what I started.

Von's dad pulled his wife away and Von walked over to me.

"I should have warned you that they're kind of different. Not like your typical parents."

I had no comments for his ass because they were indeed different. He got closer to me and just looked into my eyes.

"You okay?"

"Yes, we'll talk later."

"Aight, I love you."

I smiled because it was good to hear him say it without me saying it to him first.

"I love you too."

"Did I just hear you two say that you love each other?" His father asked.

Neither of us responded. His father asked to speak with him in private and I just knew it was about me. Tanah resumed what she was doing and looked at me and smiled.

"You're so pretty. I know my son, so I know the two of you are intimate, so I hope that you two are practicing safe sex."

If only she knew that I was on birth control and didn't plan to get off any time soon.

"Yes, ma'am."

"Good, and don't call me ma'am, I'm not that old."

We laughed, and I finally felt a little better. She eased up on the questions and talked more about Von growing up. I laughed because he hadn't changed with his boss attitude.

After I finished the task she gave me, she prepared the rest of the food. It took her about an hour to finish everything. We set the table and she told me to go get the men. She guided me on how to find her husband's man cave. When I walked in the direction, there were just a few steps before I would actually step foot into the room. I paused for a moment after overhearing my name.

"Now that you're finally off your call, I have something to ask," his father mentioned.

"Okay, ask."

"Son, you can't be serious about LoVonna?"

"What you mean I can't be serious about her?"

"She's what nineteen or twenty?"

"She's twenty, and she's grown as hell. She ain't out here like them other chicks, she got a good head on her shoulders. She's in school to be a physician, and she got straight A's. My lil' baby is the real deal."

"That just proves she's not the one for you. I can see it in her eyes. She's one of those goody two-shoes type of bitches. She'll land your ass a life sentence in prison. I'm telling you to get rid of her now."

"How can you even fix your mouth and say some shit like that. Lo knows what I'm into. She doesn't judge me."

"I bet she probably thinks you're going to eventually get out the game, is that what you told her?"

"Pops, you tripping for real."

"She's not the one, and I don't like nor care to have her around. Layla is who you should be with."

When he said that, those words hit my heart like a sniper hitting his target. I felt tears forming in my eyes. I didn't even have a full conversation with him, and he was saying all types of things about me.

"She is the one. Have I ever brought a woman over here? Hell nah, I never even introduced you to Layla. Layla never even been to my big ass house. We stayed in the other one, so tell me how she is the woman for me."

"Layla is a rider, she's been down with you from day one. She has your son, build a family and foundation with her. If you want to keep fucking this LoVonna girl, then do just that, but don't make her your woman."

I had heard enough, so I made some noise coming off the step.

"Hey, your mom told me to tell you two that the food is ready."

"Aight, lil' baby, we'll be right there."

My appetite was ruined, and I just wanted to leave and go home. His mom asked was everything okay when I came back and I asked her where the restroom was. Once inside the restroom, I splashed cold water onto my face because the tears had already started and I knew my eyes would be red.

Once I made it out of the restroom, I came back and met them in the dining area. Von had a mean look on his face, and his mom didn't look pleased either. His father on the other hand had been looking like he wanted to kick me out, so his facial expression didn't matter.

"You okay?" his mom asked again."

"Oh yes, I'm good. I can't wait to eat. Should I bless the food?" I asked, lying about waiting to eat.

"We don't bless the food around here. We just eat," his father stated.

"It's okay, I've always wanted to bless the food, go ahead, LoVonna," Tanah told me. I blessed the food quickly and we started to eat. I took small bites because I didn't have an appetite at first, but after tasting how good the food was, I started to smash some shit.

After dinner, I helped Tanah clean up. Von was standing close by and his father was nowhere to be seen, and I was actually happy. Hearing how he felt about me let me know he didn't want me around. I planned to never go to his home again.

"I love you Trigga, you take care of that cute girl," his mom said, hugging him.

"I will," he replied back.

Tanah hugged me and told me to stay in touch. I told her that I would, even though I didn't plan to. She was cool, but I couldn't see myself being around her. We took off and before he could turn in the direction of his home, I asked if he could take me to my mom's house."

"Did you leave something there?" he asked.

"No, I think I'll stay with her tonight."

"I thought we were going to watch your favorite chick flick and fuck?"

"I just want to spend time with her before I leave. My father isn't home and it's rare when it's just her and I."

"What's wrong with you, did my mom say something to offend you?"

Yes, the bitch said a lot of shit, but she's not the fucking problem!

I tried my best to keep my tears intact.

"LoVonna, tell me if she did, and I will confront her about the shit."

"Your mom didn't say shit, Trigga. Just drop me off, please."

"Trigga? That just let me know you mad about something."

I tried to reason with him, but my feelings were hurt. I was scared and confused because after that, I didn't know where our relationship would stand.

He pulled up to my mom's and I got out.

"Lo?"

"Yes," I answered, turning around.

"I know you ain't about to get out of this car without talking to me."

"I'll call you tomorrow. I just..." I said as I stepped back into the car. I couldn't even make up a lie, because I was really hurt. I knew I had to tell him that I heard what his father said about me.

"Whatever it is, I wish you would just tell me."

"We'll talk later."

"I have to get Layla's car fixed. She don't have no fucking money, and it's in the shop. I wouldn't give a fuck if Volante wasn't involved."

I don't know why hearing her name pissed me off even more. His father wanted him to be with her, maybe he should.

"Yeah, you handle that," I told him. I kissed his cheek and got out of the car. I shut the door and he pulled off. I knew he was pissed, but so was I.

"What happened?" my mother asked, walking into my room. She was doing some work when I came in, so I didn't bother her. I bathed and just laid down.

"His parents are different, but that's not even the bad part. After over hearing his father say all types of things about me, I don't even know if I want to still be with Von."

"What? What did he say?" she asked, now sitting on my bed.

I told her everything I heard him say and she was just pissed as I was. But she reasoned and told me what she felt I should do.

"Your grandpa couldn't stand your father either. But that didn't stop me from loving him. I told you about your father's past, and I'm not ashamed of that. You damn sure can't be ashamed of what you have. LaVondrius' father had no right saying that about you, but you can't please everyone. I think his father has some issues within himself. Don't stop loving LaVondrius because of how his father feels about you. Now, if he didn't defend you that would be different."

"Thanks, Mom," I told her, hugging her.

"Anytime, doll."

She left, and I just laid there thinking about what was to come.

NEEN

I was so scared as I stared at the pregnancy test that read positive. I wanted to tell E, but I wanted the doctor to confirm it first. I wanted to give him a son. I was scared because losing another child consumed my mind. I didn't know how I would make it through.

Risa and Vonna were on their way over. I had tossed the pregnancy test away and cleaned up. They were heading back to school in a few hours, so I wanted to spend some time with them. It wasn't long before they were ringing the doorbell.

"Do y'all always have to look so cute?" I asked them.

"Yeah, duh," they both said in unison.

I looked at Risa and smiled because I knew that her and Diggy were back together and on good terms.

"I still can't believe your damn uncle did that shit," Risa stated.

"I can, that's just who he is. He didn't care that the shit would hurt you. He can't even use it as an excuse in protecting you."

"I'm over it. I don't plan to hold a grudge, but I can't see myself having father-daughter time anytime soon."

"I hear that, but—"

I stopped when I heard E and Trigga come into the house. E had told me he was gon' be out for a while taking care of business. He walked over to me and kissed my lips. He then headed straight into the kitchen. By his eyes being low, I knew he was high as fuck.

"Yo' ass over here, like I ain't been calling you all fucking morning!" Trigga yelled at Vonna.

"I was going to call you. I been with Risa all morning."

"So, what the fuck you on? I'm not about to sit around and wait for you to leave a nigga like you did before."

"Can we talk about it later?"

"Fuck all that. You tell your girls everything else. Just like last night, you called Risa and told her you didn't know if our relationship would last," he stated. I looked at Vonna and knew she didn't want to talk about it in front of us.

"Let me show you this outfit, Risa."

We headed to my room and we both felt bad. I also knew that Vonna was second guessing their relationship because of Trigga's father.

Inside my room, I went to my walk-in closet. It was more like a room because it was big as hell. I showed her the outfit and she smiled wide.

"Oh my God, cuz, I love you so much. My twenty-first birthday gon' be lit ass fuck."

"Yes, it is. Don't show Diggy this dress. I don't want him coming at me sideways. Once you have it on, he won't trip because he'll be too busy drooling over how good you look."

"You damn right," she said with a smile.

I peeped out into the hall, making sure E wasn't nowhere in sight. I shut the door and stared at her as she admired the dress the designers made for her birthday. It was a red sequin cocktail dress and I knew she was gon' kill it.

"Why you close the door?" she asked, finally looking over at me.

"I'm pregnant."

"Oh my God! Congrats!"

"Shh! I didn't tell him yet. I want the doctor to confirm it. Plus, if I tell him he's going to treat me as if I'm disabled. Besides, I'm not missing your twenty-first birthday."

"Aww, what do you want a boy or girl?"

"I just want him or her to be healthy. But of course, E wants another boy."

"I bet he does. Karma a bitch out here, he better hope it ain't no girl," she told me.

I laughed because I knew exactly what she was talking about. Having a girl changes a nigga whole mindset. The shit he took me through, he would kill a nigga if they did that to our daughter.

"Girl, what the fuck was that?" Risa asked.

We heard a noise, a crashing noise like something was thrown into something else. Running out the closet and my bedroom, we headed to see what it was.

"What the fuck was that noise?" I asked E. He was looking at Vonna who looked as if she was about to kill someone.

"I'm so sorry, Neen. That nigga pissed me off to the max. I threw your kitchen stool at his ass, and the nigga tried to throw it back, but thanks to E, he saved me by stopping the chair. It was so close to hitting me."

"Where the fuck is Trigga? Why his ass throwing shit at you? What happened, because we weren't even in the room that long?"

"Aye, I'm about to go holla at that nigga before he fucks the city up. I'll call you later, ma," E told me. He kissed my lips and left.

Once he left, I sat them down so that we could talk.

"Vonna what happened? I'm not even mad about the chair, that ain't shit."

"You heard when his ass came up in yo' crib popping off at me. Well, when y'all walked away he was still coming at me hard. I was just about to tell him I overheard what his father said, but then the nigga gon' say that he ain't got time for childish games and before he chases a bitch, he'll go back to Layla."

I covered my mouth because I knew that fucked her up. I see why her ass threw the stool at him.

"Wow, did you hit him with the stool?"

"Did I? It almost knocked his ass over."

She laughed, and I had to join in.

"I hate to see y'all like this. Stop letting people interfere with what y'all have," I stated.

"Plus, my birthday coming up, and I don't need y'all beefing," Risa added.

"I'm just tired of basically fighting to be with him. It's like shit keep happening. Is it a fucking sign? Should a bitch just bail?"

"Nah, you leaving in a bit, ain't you? Go handle that with yo' nigga. Believe me, you don't want to let Trigga go. Unless you're the one breaking up with him because you don't give a fuck, your ass gon' hate to see him with another bitch."

She sighed and told us she was about to head over his house. After I called E, he told me they were going to Trigga's crib.

"Now that y'all got y'all shit out in the open," Risa stated.

"Wait, what shit Neen got out?" Vonna asked.

"Don't tell anyone, especially Trigga, but I'm pregnant."

"Wow, congrats but why is it a secret?"

"It's not, I just want the doctor to confirm it. Home pregnancy test can sometimes give false results."

"Okay, now back to me because I need advice," Risa said.

We glanced at her, giving her our undivided attention.

"Yesterday, Darcel asked me to move in with him once school is finished. But when I'm on break, he wants me to live with him. I didn't tell him no, but I didn't say yes either. Vonna, how you feel about that?"

"Girl, I'm not tripping, you deserve to be happy. I take it you're not staying closer to school once we graduate?"

"Still haven't decided yet, but he said we can buy a house wherever."

"Awww, y'all too cute, but I'm going to go holla at Von before we hit the highway. Once you move out, I can't be all lonely and shit. Let me make sure he's good."

We burst out laughing while we walked her outside. Once she left,

I talked about the baby more and also about my fears. Risa prayed with me and I felt much better afterwards. I just hope God heard our prayer.

LOVONNA

I stood at the door of Von's house. I walked in because the door was unlocked, and he never kept his door unlocked. I walked around the house and smelled that shit they always smoked on. I finally found him and his crew outside in the back, playing ball. When I walked up on Von, E and Diggy, I stopped when I reached Von. Standing in front of him, I couldn't do shit but admire how sexy his ass really was. His muscles were ripping through his wife beater.

"Can we talk?" I asked.

"Nah, we playing ball," he told me. I guess E and Diggy felt we needed to.

"Aye, y'all can have that, man, we out," Diggy spoke.

"Yeah, y'all petty motherfuckers need to stop that crazy shit," E added.

Von kept shooting the ball around not paying me any attention. I made sure E and Diggy were gon' before I walked over to Von and stole the ball from him.

"Can we talk, please, baby?"

"Oh, I'm baby now?"

"You will always be bae, Von. I just need to get something off my chest."

"The court is yours," he told me. Lifting his leg up and resting it on the chair, he leaned on his knee and stared at me while crossing his wrists over one another. I hated when he focused on me like that.

"I was just in my feelings because I overheard your father talking about me. He doesn't like me and I'm actually cool with that, but for him to just bash me without even knowing me, fucked me up. He wants you to be with Layla. How can I compete with that?"

While he was staring at me, I didn't know what he was thinking. I wanted him to just grab me and say it would be okay.

"You can't because there's no competition. I already told you, I want you and only you. If you heard what my father said, then, I'm sure you heard what I said. I don't want Layla. Yeah, I fucked up at E's crib and let that shit slip out about me being with her because I was pissed at your ass. You walking around here harboring ill feelings, but you ain't tell me shit. How am I supposed to know you were feeling like that?"

He grabbed his phone from his pocket and looked it. He looked back at me and said we could finish talking inside the house. Once inside, he stripped out of his clothing and quickly showered. I sat on the bed, just watching him get dressed into lounge around attire. He had on sweats and a t-shirt. Walking over to me, he pulled me from the bed and sat down, tugging me onto his lap.

"We ain't about to be breaking up and getting back together. I'm too fucking old for that shit, so I need to know how you really feel about a nigga."

"Von you know I love you. I'm in love with you. I just keep thinking about my father not liking you, and now your father doesn't like me."

"And? That ain't got shit to do with us. I don't give a fuck about that shit my father spitting."

"I'm sorry, Von, it won't happen again, but I'm not going over your parent's house anymore."

"I can understand that, ma. I've been waiting for Layla to give me a DNA test on Volante, but she just keeps making up excuses and shit.

But when it does happen, I want you to meet him if he's mine," he told me.

"Okay, cool, and do you really think you need one?" I asked. Volante looked just like him.

"I mean I don't, but a nigga want to be sure."

I looked down at my hands, and he turned my face toward him.

"You gon' have my babies?"

"Babies?"

"Yeah, babies."

"Not any time soon, but when and if I do, it'll be one, playboy."

"Playboy my ass, I'm shooting twenty of them fuckers up in you."

I snorted so hard because I knew his ass was lying. He had already told me in the beginning he wanted one or maybe two children.

"But check this out, I don't need your little ass throwing tantrums and running over your momma house just because someone said something about you. My father ain't shit, so you shouldn't even take that shit serious. But other than that, how you feel about my moms and shit?"

"Your mom was cool after she stopped asking so many questions, but I think she thinks I'm a spoiled brat that has it easy."

"Well, I don't know if you realized it or not, but you are a spoiled brat and you do have it easy."

"Shut up." I punched him in the arm when we heard his doorbell ring. I got up and let him answer. After a while I, headed down and I heard why it was taking him so long to come back up to the room.

"Son, I just stopped by to see how you were doing," Volante said to him.

"I'm straight pops, just chilling with my girl."

"That's her car out there?" Volante asked.

"Yes."

"Umm, she got money."

I walked back toward the room but didn't go all the way in. I wanted to eavesdrop.

"That's not even your business."

"You're right, where is she?"

Oh hell nah, do not bring that crazy motherfucker up to this room! I thought.

Next thing I knew, I heard my name being called. I closed my eyes and walked out the room and down the stairs. Once I got closer to them, I just stared with no expression.

"LoVonna, you're looking beautiful as ever. It's good seeing you again."

Man, get your ole' fake ass out of here.

"Really, I thought for some reason you didn't like me."

"What would give you a reason to think that?" he asked.

I wanted to snap on his old ass, but I kept it together and stayed respectful because I was taught to never disrespect my *elders*.

"I'm not sure. I guess the vibe I feel when I'm around you."

"Is that so? Well, my son here seems to be really fond of you, and I can see why. You're very beautiful."

I looked over at Von, and he looked at his father as if he hated him. After standing there in silence, I finally excused myself and told Von I was about to go. I wanted to spend more time with him, but I couldn't stand to be around his father.

"You leaving me already?" Von asked. His father damn near snapped his neck, looking over at Von.

"Just thought I'd give you two some space."

"He's leaving. So, ain't no point in you going anywhere."

His father didn't seem too pleased that his son was kicking him out, but I was in fact, beyond happy.

"Well, I do have other errands to run, LoVonna," he said, nodding at me.

Once he left, Von locked up and pulled me into his arms.

"I will tell you this, I'm tired of not being able to see you when I want to," he revealed.

"I know, but if we both do what we should, we can make it work."

"Yes, we can, when do you have another break?"

"I'll be done in three months for the year but my residency program starts. I have to study for the NCCPA exam. I pray I pass that. It's so much work. There are several things I have to accomplish or obtain before I can practice the full scope of a physician."

"I thought medical school took at least four years, has it changed?" he asked.

"No, I damn near triple my classes and I had all advanced classes in high school. Many of the college courses were excluded from my rotation because of that. The residency is three to eight years."

"Damn, my lil' baby smart like that?"

"Yeah, something like that." I looked up at him, and he knew what I wanted.

"You want daddy? Don't you?"

"Yes, I need you to break me off proper before I head back."

He kissed my lips and walked backwards with me as we headed toward the steps. I finally felt that nothing could get in the way of our love. Some may say it was too soon to have strong feelings for one another, but when you know, you just know. Six months couldn't define our love for one another.

NEEN

$\mathcal{T}$he pregnancy test came back positive. The doctor confirmed it. I had a nice dinner planned for E and I. Once I was dressed, I waited on him to put his shoes on.

"You look beautiful, baby," he told me.

"Thank you, you look nice as well."

"Well, when my girl tells me she got something special planned for a nigga, I had to jump fresh."

Once inside the car, I pulled out the garage. I couldn't contain myself, because I was so happy, and knew he would be just as happy.

We ended up at Vestia. Vestia's was one of the restaurants Diggy and Trigga own. I loved the Italian food that was served there. Once we were seated and the manager noticed us, he took our orders right away. Jim always went out of his way when we came in. I think he just wanted us to report back to Diggy and Trigger about how good he was doing.

Once our food was out and we took a few bites, I handled E an envelope. He looked at it and then back up at me.

"What's this?" he asked, opening up the envelope I had given him.

"Open it and see."

"You'll see ten little fingers. Ten little toes, but less time to meet me, how about seven on the nose?"

I beamed with joy when he read over it again, trying to figure out what it meant.

"Okay, ten fingers, ten toes… Seven on the nose. What the hell that mean?"

"It means seven months."

"I'm not getting it, so seven months. Ten fingers, ten toe… toes."

He got quiet and looked into my eyes. I shook my head up and down while smiling. I pulled the home pregnancy test out and gave it to him.

"Neen, don't even play like that."

"I'm so serious. I'm two months. In seven months, you'll be a father."

I expected for him to be happy, but he jumped from his seat and came over to me.

"You don't know how happy this shit makes me. Have you started prenatal care, what the doctor say?"

"E, calm down. She said that everything is fine. They will do more tests later down the line, but we're going to pray and everything is going to work in our favor. Our child will live to bury us."

"I don't even wanna finish eating, I'm ready to get you home and do somethings to your ass. You giving me another child means every-thing to me. I know how scared you are, but we got this baby."

"With you by my side, I know everything will be okay. Are you serious about leaving?" I asked.

"Hell yeah!" He yelled for the check, and Jim ran right over. After paying, we headed home.

Inside the car, we talked more about the baby.

"I just want a healthy baby, but if I had to choose, I would say a boy," he told me.

"I want a girl," I told him.

"I don't know, if she is beautiful like her mom, I don't have time to be killing niggas out here over mine."

"You are so crazy. That'll serve you right."

"Nah, it wouldn't."

We laughed and continued to head home. I sat in silence, thinking about the baby. I knew another child wouldn't replace our son EJ, but it would bring joy that was much needed.

Pulling into the garage, I noticed E was focused on his phone. He was texting away, with a serious look on his face. I knew it had to be business from the way he was looking.

"Everything okay?"

"Yeah, shit straight."

Walking into the house, we got settled, and then cuddled on the couch.

"So, if it's a boy, do you feel comfortable letting him wear some of EJ's old attire? Especially the custom shoes Trigga got made for him when he was first born. It's a lot of shit the designers customized for him. What do we do with it?"

"If we do have another boy, I would love for him to wear some of EJ's things. It would bring pleasant memories."

A tear rolled down my face, and he wiped it away. Losing a child was the hardest battle I ever had to face. I was still dealing with the pain, but every day was a healing process.

"I know it's a daily struggle, but we have done so well. EJ is still a part of our lives. He's looking down on us. When our child comes into the world, he or she will have their big brother watching over them. We have an angel, Neen, watching over us."

E always knew the right things to say to make me happy. It was him and my mother that helped me continue on with life when EJ died. Although E and I had our issues with him cheating, he was still a great father.

"I love you, E."

"I love you more, now let's see if I can put two babies in you."

DARCEL

$\mathcal{I}$ was meeting the crew for an important meeting I put together. Trigga wanted to meet before the meeting, so I came a little early.

"Sup, fool?" I asked him.

Walking into our big ass room, it was kind of designed like a conference room but we didn't have nothing major inside of it. Normally, niggas in the street would use a warehouse or stash house to meet. But that was minor shit. We were some kings out here in the streets. The office was inside of one of Trigga's houses. He had three, which I thought was crazy as hell but I found out down the line,that they were beneficial for our meetings and businesses.

"Just wanted to talk with you before the meeting. I know you been doing your thing and you're probably ready for a nigga to take back over, however, I think you doing the damn thing. Unless you really want me to take over, I think I'll handle shit from behind the scenes. Although, we can work side by side."

"Yo, you serious, nigga?" I asked.

"Hell yeah."

"What about your pops, nigga?"

"Fuck him. How would he know if I'm not in control or not? I'll put the word out there, but I'm letting people know they still have to answer to you."

"Aight, I'm with it bro. Shit, like you said, we work side by side."

"What it do?" E asked, walking into the room.

"Man is this nigga really glowing?" Trigga asked.

"Hell yeah, he is."

"Chill out with that shit, but what's good?" E asked.

"Just hollering at Diggy being in charge."

"Shit, he been running shit, what's new?"

Trigga chuckled and I looked down at my ringing phone. It was Nivea. When we exchanged numbers at the skating rink. I called her maybe once. Up until a week ago, she had been calling non-stop. I would cut her short and tell her I had to go. I told her I had a girl, but she wanted to remain friends. She even gave me advice on how to keep Risa happy.

The meeting was in full swing. Only our top twelve soldiers were allowed to attend the meeting. Our connect was in attendance and we required them to attend one meeting a year. The others were people we had on payroll.

"Saliburry, you pull that shit again, just know we will end your fucking career," I snapped. I was still pissed he told Risa that shit. I didn't give a fuck how close him and her father was.

"Look, let's not forget that I'm a detective here," he stated.

"Anyway, I just want y'all to know that Diggy will still be in charge. I'll still oversee everything, but I think we can all agree that he's doing the damn thing," Trigga announced, not giving a fuck about what Saliburry was saying.

Everyone agreed that me staying in charge wasn't a problem. We were just wrapping up our meeting when Trigga's father walked in.

"Well, I see a meeting was held today. Why wasn't the legend invited?" Volante asked.

All of the soldiers stood up and straight as if they were showing him a sign of respect. I chuckled seeing that shit get under Trigga's skin.

"A meeting was held for my empire," Trigga specified.

"Well, I guess that means that you've announced that you're back in charge, right?"

I waited to see what Trigga's response would be.

"Indeed, it was."

"I guess I'll have to find out myself."

He stood before our soldiers and looked into their eyes.

"Who is in charge?" he asked them.

They all pointed at Trigga like the trained men they were. I smiled at the loyalty I felt passing through the air. They respected Volante, but they feared Trigga and respected him more. It wasn't long before he left after chatting with us a bit more.

Heading out the door, my phone rang and it was Nivea.

"Yo, that's Risa calling?" Trigga asked.

"Nah, Nivea."

"Nigga, you still entertaining that hoe? Risa gon' fuck your ass up."

"It ain't even like that; we're just friends."

"Friends?" he and E both asked.

"Look, what y'all getting into tonight? I'm trying to hit the casino up," I asked, changing the subject.

"We can do that. Lo ain't fucking with a nigga this week. She been stuck in them books," Trigga revealed.

I knew his ass was missing her."

"Shit, Risa been on the same shit. I talked to her once today."

"Her birthday in what, three weeks?" E asked.

"Hell yeah, and I'm trying to figure out what to do. She already said she don't wanna turn-up in no club for her twenty-first birthday. So, I'm thinking about a trip out of the country or a cruise or some shit."

"Hell yeah, she'll like that."

"Vonna would too. You know she gon' want them there as well."

"Aye, you know what? I could use a vacation. Make that shit happen my nigga. Let me know the details, so I can tell Lo. You know she need notice for every damn thing."

"How far is Neen, you think she straight to travel?" I asked E.

"She's three months now. She's good, but like this nigga said, let me know."

"I got y'all. Let me get home and plan some shit out."

We split and went our separate ways. Nivea called again, so I answered.

"Sup? You been blowing a nigga up all day."

"I wanted to personally invite you out somewhere," she said. "Where?"

"To my friend's party. She just passed the bar to become a lawyer."

"All damn, that's what's up. I think I'll pass though."

"Aww, Diggy, come on. It'll be fun, plus I want to see you."

I knew I was playing with fire, and the shit could blow up in my face. Yes, I was attracted to her at first, but we became friends. After I told her I had a girl, she didn't take it there with me, and I respected her for that.

"I don't want to see your crazy ass," I said with a chuckle.

"Whatever, well can we meet for lunch tomorrow?"

"Look, we cool and everything, but I just don't think my girl would be cool with all of that."

"Oh, well, I mean she can come. We are friends, plus I'm seeing someone."

"Yeah, she's crazy as hell. She won't go for that."

"Umm... well, I guess I'll talk to you later."

She ended the call, and I knew I had to cut all losses with her. I wasn't trying to make shit complicated when it didn't need to be.

After going home and changing my clothes, I looked into a few trips for Risa's birthday. I found a few places I knew she would like.

I was pulling up to the casino with E and Trigga. We were on the East side of Los Angeles. The Commerce casino was the spot to gamble at. Walking in, I roamed toward my favorite Blackjack table.

"Yo, we about to go play Three Card Poker," Trigga stated.

He and E walked off, and I got comfortable, ready to tear some shit up.

After sitting and playing Blackjack for about an hour, I got up and cashed in. I was up $20,000, and I had only started with $500. That's one hell of a profit. After collecting my shit, I put the money in my Louis Vuitton bag and walked off.

"Sup?" This nigga Muff asked me. Muff was the same nigga at the pool party that was trying to get Neen and the girls to play ball in the pool. Trigga shut that shit down. I still remember his exact words.

"Throw that fucking ball and your arm will be thrown through your mama's fucking window!"

I walked off not saying shit to him or his niggas. I saw the look in their eyes. I wasn't timid about shit.

"I see you still hostile about that shit at the pool party. What you gon' beat every nigga ass that tries to holla at your girl? She fine as hell though, I wouldn't mind having her legs wrapped around me while I'm beating her shit up."

I knew he wanted a rise out of me. I wasn't tripping off the shit he was spitting. While he was dreaming of fucking my girl, I was the one who was sexing on her good. I chuckled and kept it to moving.

"Be smooth out here. I would hate for that bag to get snatched," one of his boys stated.

"A nigga ain't that stupid to snatch shit of mine, even if I left the bitch sitting on a table."

Not caring to indulge in anymore shit they had planned out, I left. I knew what they were up to.

Walking up to E, I saw he was racking some shit up just from looking at the poker chips he had stacked up. I knew he was up about fifty thousand.

"Where Trigga at?"

"Sitting his gay ass over there caking with Vonna on the phone." He chuckled.

I laughed and walked over to Trigga sitting down at a table. He had a drink next to him. His head was cocked to the side, looking at his phone. I saw Vonna looking happy as ever.

"Sup, sis?" I asked her.

"Hey, big head, I'm surprised you ain't come up here."

"Been handling shit, but I'll make it out there soon. Ya' girl tripping?"

"Nah, she just misses you. All she talks about is moving in with ya big headed ass."

"Stop saying my head big. That jug you got sitting on top of them shoulders way bigger than mine."

Trigga laughed and she got mad.

"Really, Von, you laughing at him roasting me?"

"Man, chill out, but like I was saying before I was rudely interrupted, try to come home next weekend. I want to spend time with you. Tomorrow we finally doing the blood test for Volante."

"That's good, I know you really wanted the test done. But I promise I'll try my hardest to come," she told him.

"Aight, I'll hit you up later, I'm gon' have you play in that pussy for me later."

"Really, Von?"

"What? I know you ain't trippin' cuz Diggy ass right here. He be having Risa doing that shit all the time," he told her.

I could see Vonna's face turning red. I laughed and she hung up on his ass.

"You a trip for that shit, but aye, why them Southside niggas in here, holding up the wall and shit? How the hell you come to the casino to stand around?"

"You already know what they on. How many was it?"

"It was six of them."

"Good, if they on some hot shit, we can split the bullets equally. You know I hate to make one feel less important for not having the same amount of bullets in their heads as the others."

"Your ass crazy."

We got up and headed back over to E. Once he cashed his chips in, we were ready to roll. We headed to the parking garage. I had already peeped them niggas following us. Commercial right? Niggas try to hit a lick at a casino, but they knew they couldn't fuck with us on that level.

"I'm just thinking how y'all niggas go without pussy for days and weeks, when y'all women away. Here I am and I already can't wait to get in between Neen's legs," E stated.

"Why you thinking about our dicks?" Trigga asked him as we walked over to my car.

"Before I answer that, I know y'all seen that shit," E pointed out.

I saw the shit way before he thought about seeing it.

"Been seen that shit," Trigga mentioned.

"Aight, but I'm just saying. I know y'all niggas. Yeah, y'all love y'all women, but I know something gotta be up," E speculated.

"If you're asking if I've cheated on Risa, I haven't. Had plenty of opportunities to do so, but she's worth way more than a night of pleasure."

I was telling the honest truth, Risa sexy ass did it for me. I got tempted, but it wasn't worth losing her over.

"On some real shit, I came close but she was on that bullshit at first. I think about it a lot, hell a nigga been locked up for years," Trigga confessed.

"Y'all niggas know what time it is."

It was that nigga Muff with his lil' crew following behind him.

We paid their asses no mind.

"Like I was saying, I was locked up for years, so when a nigga want it, he want it. But Lo pussy so fucking tight and wet. Damn, I might have to take that ride tonight," Trigga continued on.

"Y'all niggas hard of hearing?" Muff asked.

"Nah, we heard you, but I'm trying to figure out why your ass still here?"

"Came to collect, drop them bags."

"Muff, you out of all niggas know not to fuck with us. What can possibly make you think you can take anything from us?"

"How about I put a hot one in your chess?" Muff asked.

"This shit so fucking funny," E added.

"Look at how you holding the gun," Trigga told him.

"You worried about how I'm holding this gun, when you should be worried about if I'm going to—"

Trigga snatched the gun so fast from his ass, even I almost missed it. I done seen him do it plenty of times to niggas.

"That's what separate men from boys. You out here trying to hit a lick, when your ass about to catch a fade with your own fucking gun," Trigga told him.

"Look Trigga, just let me work for you," Muff pleaded.

"Work for me?"

His ass had to been smoking that white shit.

"Yeah," Muff told him.

"I can't let a nigga like you work shit for me. You see how your niggas ain't fucking move when I took the gun from you? They don't give a fuck about you nigga, they just wanted parts of whatever you told them you were going to get from us. You think taking shit is how you make it out here in these streets?" Trigga asked.

"Is there a problem out here?" A security guard walked over and asked. We had already peeped him walking over to us.

"Nah, just schooling these youngsters, we good," E told him. He took one look at Trigga and walked away.

Trigga took the clip from the gun and gave it back to Muff's ass. He didn't even have a damn bullet in the chamber.

"Next time we cross paths, make sure you're out my way," Trigga warned.

Muff walked away looking stupid as fuck. I wanted to blow his fucking brain out. I knew the parking garage was full of cameras and I didn't need no one pointing me and the crew out in a fucking line up.

LOVONNA

I had been calling Von ass all day and he still hadn't called back. I gave up after the tenth call. I was missing him like crazy.

Inside of the grocery store, I was shopping around for organic food. A colleague of mine told me about how she loves it. I was a healthy eater, but I wasn't one that knew all about the organic food. I walked down the aisle, looking around when my phone rang.

"Hey, boo," I said to Risa.

"Where you at?"

"The grocery store, you made it home yet?" I asked.

"Yep, just got in. It was so fucking hot today."

"Who you telling? You talked to Diggy at all today?"

"Through text. Why, what's up?"

"Trigga ass ain't called me back yet."

"You know that man be busy. You want me to ask Diggy where his ass at?" she asked.

I was about to tell her yeah before I turned the corner to see his ass in the cereal aisle.

"Girl, this nigga here at the damn store. His ass must have been trying to surprise me, let me call you right back."

"Aight, I know Diggy ass better be near if Von's there."

I laughed and ended the called. I walked over to Von, his back was toward me, but I knew that nigga from anywhere."

"So, were you trying to surprise me?" I asked.

Instantly, I thought about my outfit and knew he would be pissed about the dress I had on. I didn't wear any panties, and he always told me that I wasn't about to be on niggas radar for sundress lurking. He said that's when niggas go out and look for women wearing sundresses and watch their ass jiggle. I thought he was playing, but I noticed plenty of times when I wore a dress, niggas would be staring extra hard.

"Excuse me?" the guy asked, turning around.

"I am so sorry. I thought you were someone I know."

I felt so crazy walking up to him. He did look like Von, it was actually scary. He could have been Von's twin brother.

"It's okay, whoever you thought I was must be lucky. You are beautiful, and that smile is sexy as hell."

"Thanks, enjoy your day."

I walked away, and my phone instantly started vibrating. It was Von FaceTiming me.

"Sup, beautiful?" he asked.

He was looking so damn sexy, I wanted to tell him I was coming to him.

"Why am I just now hearing from you, Trigga?"

"What I tell you about calling me that shit? I'm gon' fuck ya lil' ass up when I see you."

"When will that be because if I have to take an ass whooping to see you, I guess I'll take that loss."

"What you got on?" he asked while snickering at me.

"A dress."

"Let me see."

I lifted the phone up higher so that he could see me.

"Why you always wearing them dresses?"

"It's hot out, and you know I hate wearing clothes for real."

"You got panties on?"

"You asking too many questions when you need to be telling me why I hadn't heard from you."

"Nah, don't change the subject."

"I'm not."

I saw the guy that looked like him come down the same aisle as me.

"We meet again," he said, walking by.

"Who the fuck is that?" Von asked.

"I don't know."

"You don't know? Then why the hell he say y'all meet again?"

"Because I walked up on him earlier. I thought he was you."

"You thought he was me? How the fuck you gon' think another nigga me?"

"Baby, he just kind of look like you."

"What the fuck you doing all in his face?"

"Didn't I just tell you what happened? I wasn't in his face."

"I'll be there in a little bit."

He ended the video chat. I giggled because he was so damn crazy.

I didn't see where the guy went. I really didn't care. I found the items I needed, paid, and left.

Walking outside to my car, I saw a girl and two guys walking into the store while I walked out. Both guys were looking at me.

"Damn, you fine as fuck. That sundress lookin' right on you too, baby."

I didn't respond. I walked by them to head to my car.

"What you looking at? That's so fucking disrespectful for you to be staring at another bitch," the chick said.

They started to argue. When I got to my car, I placed the items into the back seat. On my way home, I called Risa and told her what happened.

"Girl, how the hell you think he was Trigga?"

"I don't know, but he really did look like him. When Von heard him say something to me, he just got all mad. Oh, but seeing me in my dress really got him pissed off too."

"You must want to die?" she asked.

We laughed and I continued to drive home. Once I pulled up, I told her I was outside.

Risa and I were making honey circus chicken. All the ingredients were organic.

"This is really good," she told me. There was a hard knock on the door, and I looked over at her.

"Who the fuck is that?" she asked me.

I didn't know, but I got up and looked out the window. It was Diggy and Von. It was only an hour ago when I talked with Von.

"It's Diggy and Von," I told her. Her eyes lit up and she started cheesing hard as hell.

I opened the door and Von grabbed me up, looking into my eyes. Diggy walked over to Risa.

"You wanna get fucked up, don't you?" Von asked me.

"How did you get here so fast? You been here all this time?" I asked.

"We rode on the jet."

"Jet?" Risa and I both asked.

"Yeah."

Von pulled me into my room after he removed his shoes. His cologne was so captivating, and he looked damn good. He wore his designer jeans and a red and white shirt. Once in my room, I wrapped my arms around his neck.

"I missed you."

"Fuck all that, you trying to play a nigga?"

"Are you really asking me that?"

He just stared at me as if I was to be okay with that question.

"LaVondrius, no, I'm not cheating on you. I told you what happened. I thought he was you, but he wasn't. So, he happened to see me on another aisle and that's when he said what he said."

"Anyway, get on all fours."

"What? How you go from being mad to wanting to fuck me?"

"On the real, I was never mad. I didn't like the fact you wore that dress, and I know your ass didn't have any panties on."

I kissed him to shut his ass up. Plus, he was looking so sexy at that very moment. He started taking my clothes off, and my pussy was jumping.

"I'm about to punish yo' pussy."

"Umm... please do."

Von laid back on the bed naked. The way he eyed me gave me more than enough confidence.

"Come ride me."

"I thought you were about to punish my pussy?" I asked, mocking him.

"I am, but I want you to come ride it first."

I planned to ride him, but first I wanted to lick all over his body. I took my time kissing and sucking on him. He even let me suck his nipple for a hot second before his ass pushed me back, saying that was enough. I took him into my mouth. It was like sucking on a damn arm. Von was too big and I often wondered how I took all of that shit inside of me.

"Damn, right there, lil' baby."

I started slurping, sucking, and licking until I saw his eyes roll in the back of his head. When his toes started to curl, I went in for the kill and deep throated as much of him as I could. He came all in my mouth, and I proudly swallowed every drop.

"Umm, that was good," I told him, licking my lips.

"Yo' ass wild."

I climbed onto him, positioning myself over him. I then eased down on his dick. No matter how many times he beat my pussy up, I always had to get used to his size. Slow grinding my hips like I knew he liked. He placed his hands on both of my sides.

"You know I love how you ride this dick, baby."

"I know, daddy."

As I sped up, I knew I was about to cum. I couldn't hold it any longer. He quickly turned me over and started beating my pussy up so well, I thought God came down and brought me up to heaven.

After making love throughout the night and into the morning, Von and I laid in bed. I was in deep thought about my residency.

"What's on your mind, baby?" he asked.

"I think I'm going to stay here for my residency."

"Okay, cool."

"I want to be around you more, but I have to do what's best for my future."

"I want that for you, so I'll tell you what. I'll buy us a house here."

"Even if you do, your businesses are still back at home."

"True, but my girl will be here."

"Aww, don't make me cry."

"Don't start that cry-baby shit. Tomorrow I want to take you on a shopping spree."

"You don't have to do that, baby."

"I know I don't, but I am. Plus, we need to get you some ice for your wrist, some shoes for your ride, and maybe something you can wear for me."

"You're always trying to throw sex in there. I don't need no rims on my car. I like the factory rims just fine."

"I'm telling you that your ride would look even better. Anyway, your lil' ass sucked my dick so good."

"Shut up." I punched him in the arm. I then laid back on his chest and we just talked about our future.

"Come back with me tomorrow. Well, in a few hours because it's already the next day, it's what 3 o'clock in the morning?" he asked.

"Yes, it is. I get to ride in the jet?" I asked.

"Yeah. I'll fly you back Monday morning before your class."

"Okay."

"So, I have to tell you something, but don't say shit, LoVonna."

"I won't, so tell me."

"Diggy taking Risa to the Bahamas for her birthday next week and guess who's joining them?"

"Who?"

"All of us, including Neen and E."

I jumped up because I was praying for a getaway. With school, I just didn't see it happening.

"Oh my God, I can't wait. I have to go shopping."

"That's why we're going in a few hours. Now, let's get some sleep, beautiful."

"Wait, how long will we be gone?" I questioned him.

"We're leaving Thursday right after your class."

"I don't have that class on Thursday anymore."

"Okay, I'll let Diggy know. Now go to sleep."

I snuggled closer to him. Von was my world and he came into it at the right time. It had been eight months of love. Since the first night I slept with him, I felt something for him. I'd never thought I lose my virginity to a man I just met. I knew I cuffed his ass because Neen mentioned how he used to be, but the side I see is nothing like what she said or even what others claimed.

LAVONDRIUS

*L*o and I sat beside Risa and Diggy. They had been kissing non-stop. I knew it was just the love and affection they had for one another. I, on the other hand, was in deep thought. Lo had a nigga feeling weird. I knew I loved her, so when she told me she loved me, I said it back. I wasn't sure if I was in love at first, but I felt that shit. She had a nigga gon'. She cuffed my heart, and I never thought I'd give it up so willing to another woman. My plan after I got out of prison was to fuck a bitch and send her on her way. I never thought that Lo would actually come home with me that night of my welcome home party. I was shocked when she asked a nigga to fuck her when she was a virgin. The sex was good, but I felt something else, like our souls were connected. I never wanted her to see my dark side. I could never tell her that I killed someone, hell, half of Cali niggas I offed. I wanted to show her more.

"You seem to be in deep thought, what's up?" Lo asked.

"Just thinking about us. You know what I'm into, and I know that it scares you, I just want you to know that I will never bring harm to you."

"I know you won't, Trigga."

I leaned over, kissed her neck, and bit down until she cried out.

"LaVondrius? Why would you do that?"

"I told your ass to stop calling me that."

"I'm probably bleeding."

"Girl, you ain't bleeding."

"I only call you that when I'm mad or horny. Now, I'm mad."

"Your horny ass. Didn't you get enough this morning?"

"Stop talking to me. That shit hurt." She pouted.

"You're a fucking cry-baby. Straighten up, and calm that shit down."

She didn't say shit else, but she dropped the attitude.

We just landed a little under an hour. My car wasn't too far from where we landed. After gathering all of our things, we exited the jet. Inside the car, Risa and Diggy were laughing about something. I asked what was funny, but no one said shit. I noticed Lo had a silly look on her face.

"You laughing too? What's funny?" I asked.

"Nothing, can we go. I don't like all these jets flying over us."

"I still can't believe y'all got a damn jet," Risa mentioned.

"Anytime y'all want to ride in it, just let Lance know. He will make it happen for you, and I already let him know it's cool," I told them.

I dropped Diggy and Risa off at his crib. I heard Risa tell Lo she was gon' have a talk with her dad. I knew she was still pissed with him about the shit he pulled.

It was still early but I wanted to take Lo shopping like I promise.

"You ready?" I asked her.

"Yeah, just had to change my clothes."

"I see, you just had to put a dress on."

"It's hot out, that's why."

"Come your ass on."

I walked into Shine's, it was the place where I got all of my jewelry customized.

"Hello, Trigga, I see you're back for more," Kealey stated.

"I am, I need you to get my woman right."

"Ohh, she must be special. What does she like, maybe a ring?" she suggested and winked at Lo.

"You're funny. But, not yet. Maybe in the future. I gotta see if she's worth carrying my last name."

"Ma'am, you might as well go customize my ring now, he knows I'm worth it," Lo added. I chuckled as she stood beside me.

Lo told Kealey what she wanted. Kealey drew it up, but still Lo didn't like it. I decided to take a crack at it. I took a piece of paper and started drawing as Lo told me what kind of watch she wanted. After I was done. I looked it over and showed her.

"You can draw?" she asked, surprised.

"Something like that."

"Something like it? Baby, you can really draw. This is good, real good."

"Thanks, but do you like it?"

"I love it."

"Wow, Trigga, that is nice. Why you let me waste my time drawing?"

"That's your job, but how long will it take to come back?"

"With all the details, we're looking at about two months."

"Two months? You can do me better than that," I told her.

"I'll push for one, but you already know the price will go up."

"That ain't shit new."

After buying her some earrings that she really liked we left. I took her to one of my restaurants. We ate and headed home. I didn't tell her that Volante would be spending the night with us, but I decided to let her know.

"Baby, Volante is coming over tonight."

"Okay, that's great."

"I got the test result back. I wanted to open it together."

"I'll always support you, baby."

"Cool."

When True brought my mail in, I saw the envelope and knew exactly what it was. I wanted to wait until Lo was around to open it.

"Do you have to go get him?"

"Yeah, probably or else my father will drop him off."

"Maybe you should go. I'm not really feeling your father. Today ain't the day either, I might pop off at him."

"Nah, don't do that because I'll really have to kill his ass."

We made it back to my home. Lo wanted to bathe. I told her I would take her and Volante shopping in the morning. She wanted to do some shopping online, so I gave her my card information. I told her I would be back in a lil' while. The apartments Layla stayed in were about an hour from my home.

"Hello?" Layla answered.

"I'll be there shortly. Make sure his shit is ready."

"Did you get the results yet?" she asked.

"Nah, but it should come Monday." I didn't want to tell her I had them.

"Can we talk when you come?"

"Nah, I have somewhere to be."

"It won't take long, LaVondrius."

That was my first time ever hearing her call me by my real name. I don't know why I thought that maybe something could be wrong.

"I'll call when I'm outside."

Hanging up, I thought about what it is that she could want. Her voice sounded different for some reason. But all that didn't matter.

Once I finally made it there, something told me to just go in. I got out and knocked on the door. Volante opened the door, and I just stared into his eyes. He looked so much like me.

"Hey, Dad."

"Did your mother tell you to open the door?" I asked.

"No, she's in the room."

"Never open a door without permission. Okay?"

"Okay."

I walked further into the apartment. It was decent enough, especially for her not having any money. As I walked further toward the back, I heard her talking on the phone.

"No, I'm just saying you're doing all that talking but not holding up the bargain on your end. You don't think I'm stressed over this shit?"

I couldn't hear whatever the person on the phone was saying back to her. I made my presence known, and she quickly hung up the phone without telling the person she would call them back.

"Who was that?" I asked. I don't know why, but I just felt the need to know.

"My man," she said with emphasis. I chuckled because I wasn't pressed one bit.

"Where is Volante's things, and why is he opening doors without your knowledge?"

"I told his lil' behind to stop doing that," she said, looking over at him.

"I'll talk with him."

"His things are over there, but can you give me like five minutes of your time."

I took a deep breath and told her yeah. I sent Volante to his room as we sat on her couch. I looked at her waiting for her to say whatever she had on her mind.

"I was scared when you went away. I didn't have anyone here, so I thought that Georgia was best for me and Volante. I had just found out I was pregnant. If I would have known your parents would have been there for me, I wouldn't have left. There was talk about you getting another three years added on. I just didn't want that for our child. I know you hate me, but I am truly sorry I left you the way I did. Now you're in love with someone else, and it's so hard to deal with. Yes, I moved on, but my heart will always and forever be with you."

I really didn't know what to say. Well, I did but those words wouldn't be appropriate after all the shit she just said. I wanted to say *bitch, please.*

"Look, whatever we had is over. I'm not trying to beef with you on no level. We have a child together. Stop all that extra shit, and I'll make sure he wants for nothing. Don't call my phone all throughout the night because for one, he's sleeping at that time and two, you know damn well I got a girl. You ain't gotta keep putting shit on social media about what we got going on. Stop trying to add Vonna as your friend as well. You're being messy, and it won't help shit but make me dislike you."

"I'm sorry, LaVondrius, I really am. But it's so hard seeing you with someone else. Just tell me this one thing. If you weren't with her, would you give me another chance?"

The answer was no, but I didn't know if I wanted to tell her that. I knew I shouldn't give a damn about her feelings, but I didn't want to hurt her more. I knew it was hard for her, but she fucked that up, not me.

"I don't know, Layla."

"Well, you didn't say no, so."

She smiled, and once upon on time, that smile made me want to get in between her legs. But shit changed.

"Tell lil' man I'll be waiting outside." I got up and walked out. I stood by the door waiting on him. Once he ran out, we headed to the car. I buckled him into his car seat and got in. I took off heading home.

Walking into the house, Volante asked if he still had ice cream over my house. I laughed because he knew we just restocked. His little ass loved some ice cream. I went to find Lo, and she was sitting in the living room. Our eyes locked, and she smiled once she noticed Volante standing beside me.

"Lo, this Volante. Volante, this is my girlfriend, LoVonna."

"Hi, Volante, you can call me Ms. Vonna."

"Okay, Ms. Vonna. Do you like ice cream?" he asked her.

"I love it."

He smiled, and I chuckled at the two of them. Layla texted saying he was already bathed, so, we all ended up in our night clothes watching movies.

I looked at the clock and it was a little before midnight. Volante and Vonna were both knocked out. I got up, thinking *who to take upstairs first?* I grabbed my son and took him to his room, making sure he was tucked into the middle of the bed. I turned the light off and left. I went to get Vonna, but she was already walking up the steps.

"I was just coming down to bring your little sleepy ass up."

"All I remember is watching the movie for like thirty minutes."

"Yeah, you and Volante both were sleep before the movie started good enough."

I was now face to face with her.

"You okay?" I asked.

"I'm awesome. Thanks for spoiling me today. Don't be mad when you see how much I spent."

"How much you spent?" I asked her.

"A little over $900."

"Really, Lo, that ain't shit."

"It is when it's someone else's money."

"Well, my money is your money."

"I wish."

"LoVonna, you can get whatever, baby."

She wrapped her arms around my neck. I tapped her legs so that she could jump on me. She quickly wrapped her legs around my waist. I carried her into our room. I wanted to make love to her, but I wanted to get the results of the DNA test out the way.

"You ready for the results?"

"Shit, I forgot. He looks so much like you."

Walking over to my dresser, I grabbed the paper out. Sitting next to Vonna on the bed, she rose up in an upright position. I quickly opened it up and read the results.

"He's mine," I told her.

"Congratulations, but I told you that you didn't need one."

"I know, but it's good to know for sure. Now, I can give him all of me. All of my love."

It seemed like when I said that, she got really quiet.

"I hope you know that doesn't change how I feel about you."

"I know it doesn't, Von. I know you love me. I'm just thinking how we can stay three hours away when you have a child here."

"We'll make it work. If I have to get him on the weekends every week or every other week, I will."

"I just don't want it to seem like I'm taking you for him."

"We've been through this, Lo. Let's move forward. Let me worry about the balance of that."

"Okay."

"Thank you for sticking by me, Lo."

"As long as you got me, I got you."

LOVONNA

*I*t was Wednesday, and I had just left my last class. We were leaving on Thursday to the Bahamas for Risa's birthday. I was already packed and ready to go. I had to admit, flying had taken a toll on my body. It made me exhausted.

Risa was getting her hair done. I ran into Jessica, and she wanted to get together and go out to eat.

Sitting in the restaurant, Jessica ordered a drink. I wasn't twenty-one yet, so I didn't even attempt to ask for one.

"So, what's new Jessica?" I asked her.

"Nothing really, I'm working fourteen days straight. A new girl just started, and I have to train her. She told me that she did some fucked up shit and had to leave before anyone found out what she did. I guess she lied about someone's results."

"Wow, that's crazy. She can go to prison for that shit."

"Right, she said it was her first and only time doing it. Someone paid her $50,000 to do it. Now, what I do is totally different. I'm letting them know the truth, not lying about it. But for that shit, the money ain't worth it. I hope no one finds out about that what she did."

"I hope not either."

We ate and talked more. I told her about Risa's birthday trip, and she wished she could go on one. I told her we could plan a girl's trip. After a while, we decided to leave. Risa's hair was done, and she was home waiting for me.

"Aww, friend you look so pretty," I complimented.

Her hair was down her back. It was body wave bundles that she had installed. I decided to wear a bob and it was looking flawless. After gathering our things, we headed to the location of the jet.

"Hello?" I answered my phone.

"Y'all made it to the jet?" Von asked.

"Yeah, don't you here it?"

"Nah, I don't. See you soon, sexy."

"You or Diggy picking us up?"

"Diggy is, I have some business to handle. But I'll see you back at the house. Diggy will have a key for you, keep it."

"You giving me a key to your house?"

"Yeah, I can't let you cuff a nigga without giving you the key, right?"

"You're so funny. Bye, Trigga."

I hung up. I knew that shit pissed him off when I called him that. I enjoyed the punishment though.

On the jet, the pilot mentioned it was raining. I was glad I decided to wear sneakers and not sandals. I had on a t-shirt and some skinny jeans.

"Vonna, I just want to let you know that after this school year is up, I'll be moving in with Darcel."

"Girl, didn't you say that already?"

"Did I?"

"Yes, you did. Are you nervous about it or something?"

"Nervous? Nah, I'm not. I'm just worried if you'll be okay."

"Why wouldn't I? I'm happy for you, Von says he's going to buy a house for us. I just don't see that happening with him having a son."

"I don't think that changes anything. It's more work for him because he has to make it work."

"Yeah, you're right. But have you talked to your father?"

"Remember I told you how he doesn't want to talk to me unless I'm done with Darcel."

"I can't believe he's really doing that. What about your mom?"

"She basically apologizes every time I talk to her. She bought me some stocks for my birthday, increased my credit card limit, and I don't even use their money anymore. She begged me to buy something for my birthday with it. Darcel doesn't want me to though, he feels like that's their way of trying to control me. Anyway, enough about them, it pisses me off to know that my dad would do me so dirty."

"Subject changed. Are you still giving Diggy the booty hole for your birthday?"

"Shut up, before the pilot hears you," she said.

"He can't hear us."

"I might."

"Lil' nasty ass," I said, cracking up.

We laughed and chatted until we landed. At that time, it was raining even harder. As promised, Diggy was there to greet us. He dropped me off at Von's crib. I showered and just relaxed until he got in. My phone alerted me that I had a notification from Facebook. It was a message from Layla. I rolled my eyes as I opened it. What I heard pissed me off, but that's actually why she sent it. She had asked Von if he wasn't with me, would he be with her. He didn't say yes, but he didn't say no either. Either way, I was the one he was with, so if me being out the picture was the only way she could get him, it was a done deal. She would never have him.

LARISA

*D*arcel was in the gas station when his phone started vibrating. The number wasn't stored in because no name showed. It rang three more times. I felt something wasn't right, so I stored the number in my phone. When he got back into the car after pumping the gas, he handed me some snacks he had gotten.

"You phone has been ringing non-stop," I told him.

"Well, it isn't ringing now, so it did stop."

"Boy, shut up."

"You know I'm all man over here. I know you know that for a fact, the way I be having your ass screaming."

"I just be faking it."

"Can't nobody fake that shit. The way I be having yo' ass screaming and them legs be shaking. Quit frontin', Risa."

Cocky ass.

I didn't say shit, because he was right. I was addicted to his loving, and I wanted it every chance I got. His phone rang again, and he just ignored whomever it was. That really made me wonder.

"Why does it have to rain?" I asked, no one in particular. Darcel and I had just pulled up to his home. Master ran over to me with his wet paws, getting me all dirty.

"Master, you're getting me dirty."

He looked at me like he didn't give a damn. Darcel took him to the back. He had built him a nice doghouse. I wouldn't even call it a doghouse because I could stand inside of it. It was so nice inside.

I decided on a quick shower. I placed the shower cap over my hair and took care of my business. It wasn't long before I felt a cold breeze hit my back side, making me quiver a little. I quickly turned around to see Darcel with a look in his eyes. He licked his lips and I knew what time it was.

"You want some company?"

"Depends on where the company trying to go."

"In you."

I licked my lips, peering down at his dick. I often wondered how I took that all in inside of me.

As Darcel kissed all over my body, he quickly picked me up and held me against the shower wall. My legs were wrapped around his waist.

"You so damn sexy, baby. This pussy gets better and better," he cited.

I couldn't respond because he was hitting my spot. I closed my eyes as I latched onto his lips. His tongue entered my mouth and I welcomed it. Sucking on it, I thought about how amazing our sex was, and I couldn't imagine having it with anyone else.

"I'm cumin', daddy."

"I know, baby, I'm cumin' with you. Shit, this pussy so fucking wet!" he yelled out.

Once we caught our breaths, he eased me down off his dick. I really didn't want to get off, but I decided to save more for later. I washed him up, and he finished washing me up.

Inside the bedroom, his phone vibrated against the dresser. I wasn't insecure, but I have never known him not to answer his phone. *Fuck it, if he won't answer, I will.* Walking over to the dresser, I picked the phone up and answered it. Darcel was facing the other way, so he didn't see me. He was busy putting a pair of boxers on, but when I said hello into his phone and put the caller on speaker, he froze.

"Hello?"

"Hello, can I speak with Diggy?"

"Yo, you answering my phone now?"

I know his ass didn't just ask me that shit.

I ignored him because he had me fucked up. I wanted to see just who the bitch was on the phone.

"He can hear you, I have him on speaker."

"Okay, Diggy, can you hear me?" she asked.

I stared at him. I wanted to do so many violent things to him. I really had to count to ten inside of my head.

"Yo, Nivea, what is it?"

Nivea? So, he does know this bitch.

"Sorry, if I caught you at a bad time, but I just wanted to see if you wanted to go skating later. I mean, it is your skating rink, and you're hardly ever there. I know it's probably because you can't skate, but I'll teach you."

Is this bitch serious?

Although I was listening to her every word, my eyes never left his. I saw every signal his body gave that he was doing me wrong. If he hadn't slept with her, he was going to.

"I already told you I got a girl, and she wouldn't like that shit."

"Just call me later," she told him and hung up.

Not one time did he look at me. He looked at the phone like the phone had betrayed him. I went back and forth with my thoughts about how I should react. I wanted to pop off and beat his ass, but what would that solve? As much as it hurt me, I had to let him explain.

"What was that?"

"It wasn't shit," he said, finally looking at me for a quick second before he turned around. Before he could even walk away, I grabbed his arms.

"Tell me, Darcel, who is she? I heard everything she said, so it's best you tell me everything."

"Look, it's really not what you think. I got her number while you and I were broken up. I called and chatted with her a few times, that's it."

"Were you two still talking while we were together?"

"Risa, it ain't what you think."

"Let me be the judge of that. You ain't helping my thoughts one bit by saying it ain't what I think. So, I'm going to do this for your Diggy. I'll give you one more chance to tell me who the fuck that bitch is before I walk up out of this house for good."

"You already thinking a nigga did something, so why explain?"

"Wow, you know what? You can have that. I'm out." I finished getting dressed. I texted Neen to come get me, and she was already coming over with E.

Downstairs, I had my bags by the door. Darcel never came downstairs, and I knew right then and there that he was up to no good. He had the right one.

When the doorbell rang, I quickly jumped up from the couch to open it.

"What y'all into for now?" E asked.

"I'm sure he'll tell you."

He walked further in and Neen looked into my eyes. Yes, I was hurt. But that's exactly why I never wanted to be in love. Every nigga that tried to talk to me, would have to blame him for fucking it up for them.

"What happened?" Neen asked.

"Girl, we're at the gas station and his phone started ringing back to back. So, when he gets into the car, I told him. He just ignores it, even when the person had called again. Once we got back here, we showered and fucked of course. He's getting his clothes on and his phone vibrates, so he had to turn the ringer off and put it on vibrate. He never turned around to see who it was that was calling, so I answered and put it on speaker. The bitch asked for him. That's not the worst part. His ass gon' ask me why I was answering his phone. I gave him a chance to explain, but all he said was that I wasn't going to believe him."

"Damn, I mean he could have at least told you who the fuck she was."

"It's cool, you know me. He wanna play, let the games begin."

"You are truly my cousin," she said, chuckling.

"My birthday is now ruined."

"Nah, we're still going. I love Diggy, but I told his ass not to hurt you. We about to turn up and show out."

"You ain't showing shit, don't forget your ass is pregnant," E said, walking into the living room. I looked around and Darcel wasn't with him.

"Where is Diggy ass at?" Neen asked.

"He up there."

Neen walked off and headed toward the stairwell. I shook my head because Darcel really showed he didn't give a fuck.

"Let me holla at you real quick," E said. I followed him into the kitchen. I sat at the breakfast bar while he stood.

"You out of all people know how females can be. He ain't messing around with that chick. He feels like telling you won't make a difference because you won't believe him any damn way. I think you need to talk with him on some real shit, leaving won't solve nothing."

"He let me leave, he's a grown ass man. That's all he talks about in the bedroom, but you ain't man enough to communicate that to me? Fuck all that, it ain't shit. I can easily find another nigga that's able and willing to communicate like a grown ass man."

"Fuck you mean find another nigga?" Darcel asked, walking into the kitchen.

"Do you want to talk or not. I'm not about to play these games with you, you acting like the bitch in the relationship."

I regretted those words as soon as they left my mouth. He rushed over to me, but Neen held him back and E stood in front of me.

"Y'all can leave," He told them.

"I'm not leaving you to put your hands on my cousin."

"I'm not gon' touch her, but she wanna act like a nigga, I'll treat her ass like one."

"Calm down, bro, let me holla at you." E pulled him away.

I exhaled when I didn't even know I was holding my breath.

"Girl, that mouth is reckless," Neen told me.

116

"I know, that's why I hate arguing with him because I can't control it."

"What is it that you want to understand about the female? If he says she's just a friend, then what? What if he says he don't know her? What if he says he was feeling her, but knew he didn't want to hurt you? I'm asking all these questions because it was shit I dealt with. The truth gon' hurt, a lie gon' hurt, so just make sure you're ready for whatever it is you're looking for."

I thought about her questions, and I didn't know. I guess deep down inside, I wanted to know if he was cheating on me.

"I'm not going to bow down because of what I might find out. Shouldn't no female be calling my man. If you want to creep, at least keep your side bitch in line. If I had a side nigga, he wouldn't be able to call me. I would call him when I want some dick. If he does happen to call and my man answer, he better hang up or say he got the wrong number. Darcel know who the fuck she was. He said the bitch's name. Apparently, he met her at the skating rink while we weren't together. I'm not tripping about that, but why the fuck is she still calling?"

"Good question, but leaving won't solve shit."

"He was willing to let me leave. I'm still fucking here, and his big-headed ass could have been told me who the fuck she is."

"I get that, but the only reason I came because we were already on our way. I'm not taking you nowhere. You're going to work it out with him. He ain't gon' touch you because he knows I'll fuck him up."

I just shook my head. I knew my cousin wasn't weak, but I wasn't gon' tolerate that shit from no nigga.

I was still sitting in the kitchen when Neen and E left. E had stopped by to smoke with Darcel. I didn't know where Darcel was at inside the house. I got up and noticed that my things were still by the door. I walked into the movie room, looking down. When I looked up, he was coming out.

"I love you, Re."

"Do you?"

"You can't question that."

"I just need to know."

He pulled me onto one of the many recliners he had. I sat on his lap, as he placed my hands into his and he started talking.

"When Nivea and I exchanged numbers, I thought she'd be someone that I would fuck and pass over, but you and I ended up back together. I never fucked her, but we did still talk. Sometimes text."

"Why?"

"Why what?"

"Why would you continue to talk and text with her?"

"I don't know, I felt like we were friends. I told her about you and everything. Now, she just calls and asks me to chill with her."

"You better end whatever y'all got going on tonight."

"I will."

I still had my guards up, I was gon' watch his ass.

"I'm going to make dinner while you handle that."

"Aight, but don't ever in your fucking life come at me like you did earlier. Especially around others. You almost got fucked up."

"Whatever, just go handle your business. Tell the bitch I said 'hey' too."

"Quit being messy."

"I'll show you messy, and your ass is still on thin ice."

I walked away to prepare dinner. I wanted to listen, but I needed him to handle it and fast.

NEEN

"*Y*ou okay?" E asked me. He acted like I was already nine-months. We were on the jet on our way to the Fort Lauderdale. Once we got there, we were getting on a boat to the Bahamas. Lance was a great pilot.

"Yes, baby, I'm good."

I stared at Risa and Diggy. They weren't talking much and I didn't know if they made up or not. I told Vonna about it and she told Trigga. We all stared at them wondering what was up.

"Do you see how they're staring at us?" Risa asked Diggy.

"Yeah, what the fuck y'all looking at?" Diggy asked.

"Just wondering if y'all cool?" Trigga asked.

"Yeah, why wouldn't we be?"

Darcel looked from me to Vonna, then E to Trigga."

"Y'all pillow talk too much. I can't tell if y'all be fucking because too much talking is going on."

"Nigga, shut that shit up. I was fucking Vonna all night and this morning. Volante almost walked in on us."

Everyone started laughing.

"Really, Von?" Vonna asked.

"Anyway, I can't wait to turn up for my birthday. I'm getting stupid drunk," Risa interrupted.

"No the hell you're not! I don't have time for your drunk ass to be doing the most out here," Diggy told her.

She whispered in his ear and he smiled back at her, licking his lips. Their freaky asses were too much.

E rubbed my stomach while talking in my ear as well about him wanting a boy. I smiled because I wanted to give him one. Even though I wanted a girl, giving him a boy was worth his happiness.

"We're coming into some heavy rain," Lance told us.

I got closer to E. I had rode in the jet many times and flew a lot on planes as well, but I never liked turbulence.

"What the fuck?" Trigga asked as we felt a hard shake, followed by another one.

"Just turbulence. We'll be out of it in a few moments," Lance stated.

"Lord, please forgive me for having sex before marriage. If you get us through this alive, I promise I'll wait until I'm married to have sex again," Risa stated.

Diggy looked at her and then looked up. "God, I know you heard her, but hear me. If I have to wait until we're married to get some of that sweet pussy I love so much, please just take us all now."

I laughed so hard even though I was nervous as well.

"Man, y'all asses is crazy," Trigga told him.

"We should be good now," Lance announced.

As the rest of the ride went smoothly, I rested my head on E's shoulder and slowly dozed off to sleep.

"Hi, Mommy," I heard a voice say. I looked around and didn't see anyone.

"Mommy?" The voice called out again, it sounded like a voice I heard before. I was standing in a room with bright lights. It was like I was standing a few feet away from the sun.

"Who is that?" I asked.

"It's me, Mommy, did you forget about me?"

It was my son. My baby. I walked closer to touch him, but he stopped me.

"No, Mommy. You can't touch me. I just came to tell you that I'm taking

my sister with me. She's sick, Mommy, and it'll hurt less if she comes with me now."

"What do you mean take your sister with you? I don't have a daughter; you were my only baby."

"I have to go, just know we love you. We will continue to watch over you and daddy."

With that, he disappeared. It was crazy, he talked so well, and he still looked like the small child he was when he died. I called out to E, but I got no answer. All of a sudden, I felt a hard shake again. I started screaming because I felt as if I couldn't move...

"Neen, baby, wake up."

I opened my eyes to see E staring at me with concern all over his face. I peered around and everyone else had the same look as he did in their eyes.

"Neen, you okay?" Risa asked.

"Yeah, I was having a bad dream.

E pulled me closer, and I couldn't wait to land.

"How much longer?" I asked E.

"About ten more minutes," he told me. I knew once we were alone, he would ask me what I was dreaming about. I prayed that what my son said in the dream was only but a dream.

DARCEL

Sitting in our cabin, I sat in the chair waiting on Risa. She was changing her clothes so that we could turn-up before we made in into the Bahamas.

"You ready, bae?" she asked me.

"Girl, I been ready."

"Come zip this up for me," she requested. I got up from the chair I was on and strolled into our bathroom.

"What the fuck, Risa! You ain't wearing that hoe ass shit. Your ass is out, and I can see your nipples."

"First of all, my dress goes over this."

"Oh, well let a nigga know something."

"Why would I wear something like this out?"

She stepped into the dress, and I had zipped the back of it up. I stood back just admiring her beauty. She was it for me. Although I never cheated on her, I wanted to make her feel like she was the only woman for me.

"Larisa, you are truly beautiful. I'm so lucky to have you as mine."

"And you, sir, are quite handsome yourself."

She hugged me, and we shared a kiss that I took too far. I tried to take her dress off, but she stopped me.

"Darcel, no!

"Just let me get a quickie."

"No, your quickies turn into a love making session for hours."

"Aight, I got you later. When you're all hot and bothered, don't come my way."

"I won't."

"Yeah, we'll see."

I opened the door for us to head out, I wasn't paying attention to anything around me, but Risa. I went to grab her butt as we walked down the hall when my name was called.

"Diggy?"

Risa and I both looked up and a nigga damn near shitted in his draws. It was that bitch, Nivea. Out of all the damns boats in the fucking world, she had to be on the same one as me.

I didn't say shit because that night Risa told me to end it with Nivea, I called her up and told her what was up. She never called again, so I thought shit was good.

"Who is that?" Risa asked as I tried to continue to walk away.

"Nivea."

Risa crazy ass turned in full circle and was headed toward Nivea. I didn't know if the crew were still in their rooms, but I prayed if shit got of hand, one of them would come out and help me.

"Don't tell me you're one of those insecure females that can't stand for their man to be in the present of another beautiful woman."

"First of all, it's *presence* and never will I be insecure about another woman. However, don't ever call my man's name out again. I'm sure you heard him loud and clear when he told you that whatever fake friendship y'all had is over. Darcel has no female friends."

"Who is Darcel?" she asked her. I just shook my head. The bitch was just looking more stupid by the minute.

"Nivea, I'm going to walk away now. It's evident that I'm talking to a damn airhead."

"Evident? Airhead? Bitch, you got me fucked up, you just mad because Diggy fucked and sucked me so good."

"You wish. That dick and tongue only been on me."

"Oh yeah? Well, tell me why he has a birthmark on his right thigh. I've kissed it a few times."

I swear I felt my heart stop. Everything Nivea was saying before that point was a lie. How she knew that information was beyond me. Only two people knew that shit, and it was Risa and Trigga. I knew my girl didn't call her up and say that shit to her. I didn't know what Risa's next response would be, but I tried to speak up before she could say anything, however, I was too late.

"Birthmark? Darcel doesn't have a birthmark on his thighs. Your information seems fraud, so try again." I knew what Risa was doing, and she wasn't going to let anyone see her sweat.

Nivea looked disappointed that the information didn't hold up. She turned and walked away.

"Nivea?" Risa called out to her.

She turned around, looking as if she was pissed.

"Let this be the last time you come for my man again. The fact that you're on this boat lets me know what you're really about. If you want to make it off, I suggest you stay away from mine. Lil' stupid, lil' bitch!"

Nivea looked over at me. She walked away and I wondered what was really going on. Something wasn't right and I could feel it. Nivea had to be watched.

"Darcel, you know I don't play games. I'm not one of those emotional ass females that get upset about bitches yapping off at the mouth. Even though the information she knew about you was true, I knew I didn't tell her that shit and we both know Trigga didn't. So, what the fuck this bitch want? Is she one of those crazy bitches you'll read about in a book?"

"I'm so happy you're clam about this. I don't know where she got that shit from. I just know she has to be watched, something ain't right with her."

"Get rid of that bitch, before I do," she vowed.

She walked off leaving me standing there with my own thoughts. *She wouldn't kill Nivea, would she?*

I caught up with her, turning her toward me. The fact that she didn't take the bait, let me know she wasn't your ordinary female.

"I love you," I told her.

"I know, now let's turn-up."

As we made it outside, we noticed everyone was turning up by the pool. I walked over to Trigg, and I guess he knew something was up. We walked away from the crew.

"Say the word, and I'll blow this boat the fuck up," he sworn.

I made sure Risa wasn't paying attention. Although I wasn't trying to keep any secrets from her, but I didn't want her knowing about the shit we did in the streets. She only knew what I told her, I never let her see anything.

"That bitch Nivea here. Not only that, but that bitch knows where my birthmark is. As we both know, only you and Risa know that shit."

"Say less, my nigga. I'll handle it."

"You know something I don't?" I asked him. I knew my nigga wouldn't cross me, but I hated when he tried solving shit on his own and didn't tell the rest of the crew.

"You know me, I got you, that's all I'm going to say. Let's enjoy sis' birthday."

He walked away and headed back to the crew.

LAVONDRIUS

I don't know why, but so much shit was on my mind. One, being my son. Finding out that he was mine changed something in me. I wanted to be a better father than my father. I knew I had to get him away from his crazy mother, I just didn't know how things would work with Lo and I.

I told her that I would balance out being a father to my son and being her man. Honestly, I didn't think it would be that hard. But, if I could get him full-time, that means she's going to be in his life a lot. I could tell her a thousand times that she doesn't have to do anything for him, but at the end of the day, being with someone with kids, you're going to have some type of responsibility. I didn't want to put too much on her. The other thing on my mind was Nivea. It was years ago when Diggy told me about his birthmark. It wasn't until my father told me he had a birthmark in the same area, that I let him know that Diggy had one on his right thigh as well. I forgot what he said that shit meant, but if Risa didn't tell Nivea that shit, and I knew I didn't, that left one person. But I just wanted to know why. I had to get my peoples involved. I knew something was stirring up, I just hated I had to wait on it.

"What you thinking about?" Lo asked as she danced all up on me.

The boat was live as fuck.

"Nothing, lil' baby."

"You sure, I'm throwing it back on you and you ain't even trying to catch it."

I chuckled at her and tugged her closer to me. I kissed her soft lips as she wrapped her arms around my neck.

"I'm good, baby, I can't wait to get up in you."

"If I weren't on birth control, I swear I would be pregnant."

"We can arrange that, lil' baby."

"No, we agreed that I'll finish school first."

"I'm only fucking with you. I'm hungry as fuck, let's go eat."

We walked over to the crew, as they were tuning up. We chatted and all decided that we would go eat. The boat was big as hell. We decided last minute to get on it and sail into the Bahamas. I been on so many cruises, I lost count. It was my first time coming with a female though. Walking back inside, the women went to the restroom, well Risa and Neen did. Lo said she didn't have to go.

"What you want to eat, Lo?" I asked her.

"I want a steak," she stated.

We sat around and ate our food, Risa was taking hella shots. I looked at Diggy staring at her and snickered.

"Aight no more," Diggy told her.

"I'm not even drunk," she told him.

"It'll sneak up on your ass. I'm telling you now, that's enough. I'm not about to be carrying your drunk ass."

While they continued to go back and forth, I had to use the restroom.

"I'll be right back," I told them.

I walked off to handle my business, it didn't take me long. I washed my hands and emerged from the restroom. Someone bumped into me and I quickly looked up to tell them to watch where the fuck they were going. But nothing came out, the person staring at me looked identical to me.

"My fault player," he told me.

"Yeah," that was all I could get out.

I walked off and thought about what my mother used to always say about having a long-lost cousin. Maybe he was it. I didn't pay the shit no mind. I just continued making my way over to my crew.

"Aye, we about to go back up to the pool. The women still wanna turn up," E told me. I laughed because even though Neen was pregnant, she still was having a good time. Although we all knew she desperately wanted a drink.

I was sitting in the lounge chair next to E. We watched our women as they danced their little hearts out. Out of nowhere, I saw a nigga come up and dance up on Lo. She quickly turned around. Whatever she said, didn't make him go away, and when he grabbed onto her arm, I was already out of my seat heading over to her.

"I told you, I have a man," I heard her say.

"I heard you the first time, but I bet he can't fuck you like I can. I'll have your lil' sexy ass all on—"

I pushed his black ass into the pool. Once he came up, he was yelling he couldn't swim. I squatted down, looking at him struggle to stay afloat.

"I thought I heard you tell my girl you would have her all on something, but never will you ever have another chance to even speak to her."

The life guard jumped in and helped him out. He started talking shit but stopped when he saw my facial expression. I guess that angel on his shoulder told his ass to go the other way.

"You good, lil' baby?" I asked Lo.

"I am now."

I kissed her cheek and went back to sit down. I felt stares coming from the side of me. I looked to my left and sure enough, Diggy and E were staring a hole in my head.

"What?"

"Man, you know what," E stated.

"If that was Neen, then what?"

"I would have scared his ass off, but I—you know what, let me stop frontin'. I would have had pushed that nigga in the damn pool too."

I chuckled because I knew they would have been on the same shit.

We had finally made it into the Bahamas, and we gathered our things because we were actually staying at the resort.

Leaving off the boat, we headed to the resort where we would be staying. Walking into our four-bedroom suite, we all got settled in for the night. It was late, but the party didn't end there. It was sis' birthday and the only thing that was on her mind was having a good time.

"Aight, the party is down by the beach," Diggy said, walking into our room.

Paradise Island was our spot. We often came to fuck off and have a good time.

"We're coming now, is Risa's ass good?" I asked.

"Yeah, she just got done eating. I told her ass no more drinking until tomorrow."

I looked back to see where Lo was at. When I noticed she wasn't close by, I asked Diggy about Nivea.

"Did you see that bitch Nivea get off?" I asked,

"Nah, I didn't see her get off the boat. In fact, I hadn't seen her ass at all since Risa shut her ass down."

"Aight, I already made the call. I even got at Goo. He said she's been at the skating rink often on the weekends. He got pictures of some girl she been with."

"Aight, cool, well y'all hurry up. I'm not trying to be out all damn night. A nigga gotta get some sleep," he whined.

"Shut your crybaby ass up," Lo spoke as she emerged from the rest room. They joked around until she was finally ready.

My phone vibrated while I was walking on the beach with Lo. I saw that it was Layla. I chose not to answer. The warm breeze didn't do us any justice. I was glad I chose to wear thin linen. We found a nice spot for us to post up at. The music was roaring through the night skies and all I saw was ass shaking from every angle.

Neen brought out a cake. She lit it, and we sang happy birthday to Risa. Others close by noticed, so they came over to wish her a happy birthday. Lo started flicking up, and I knew I had two more days of that shit. She took pictures of every damn thing.

NEEN

*W*e had been back from the Bahamas two days now. I had such a wonderful time, I had taken the rest of the week off of work because I hadn't been feeling well. Sitting on my couch, my phone starting ringing, so I got up to get it from the kitchen counter.

"Hello?"

"Hey, baby, how you are?" my mom asked.

"Hey, Mom, I'm good. How are you?" I walked back to the living room and what I saw on the couch caused me to drop the phone to the floor. I reached behind me and patted my butt and felt the dampness.

"No. No. No!" I screamed out. It was blood on the couch, and I knew why. I fell to the floor and screamed. I didn't know what I did, but I felt God was punishing me.

I could hear my mother screaming through the phone, but I couldn't speak. All I thought about was losing another child. I just knew my life would never be the same.

As I laid on the floor, I heard the front door open. I don't know how long I was down there. My mom ran over to me, and E was right behind her.

"Neen, baby, what happened?" E asked.

"Neen, are you okay?" My mom asked.

"I lost it. I lost the baby," I cried. I closed my eyes tight, praying it was just a dream. As I was lifted from the floor, I could hear them talking, but nothing made sense. It was then I felt a sharp pain in my side before everything went black.

Beep. Beep. Beep.

I struggled to get my eyes open. But when I did, I saw that I was in the hospital which proved that my nightmare was a reality.

"Hey," E said, walking over to me. I couldn't even look him in the eyes. I felt like I was less of a woman because I couldn't even give my man a child.

"I'm going to give you two some privacy. I'll be down in the cafeteria getting some coffee," my mom told us. She left and E turned my face toward him.

"Look at me, Neen."

I looked up at him as a tear fell down my eyes.

"It's not your fault. The doctor said the probability would be low for us. Don't let this beat you down. We'll get through this together, baby."

"Why can't I just give you a child?" I asked, while crying.

"Neen, don't do that. Let's just pray the next time things will work in our favor."

I didn't want to tell him that I wasn't going through that again. There was no more trying.

There was a knock at the door, and I expected to see my mom walking in. It wasn't her, it was my uncle, Larell, and his bitch of a wife.

"Neen, your mom called and told us what happened. We just wanted to come and check on you," he told me.

I stared at my uncle because he was so fake. All the shit he said about me in the past lets me know how fake he really is.

"You didn't have to come," I told him. His wife stared at me with sympathy eyes.

"I know, but you're my niece, and I wanted to make sure you were doing okay."

"I'm good."

"How is your son doing?" he asked.

That question got E's full attention. I think it was time to tell him my son wasn't with us, and that he died years ago. He cleared his throat, making his presence known.

"I guess, I'll introduce myself. My name is E and I'm Neen's boyfriend."

"I know who you are, young man."

"Latrell?" my mom blurted, walking back into the room.

"Justice?" he turned around.

"Well, I see you made it. I thought for sure, you were busy."

"I'm never too busy for my niece."

I chuckled at that comment because he was really showing how fake his ass really was.

My mom introduced them to E.

She chatted with them, while E tried to assure me it wasn't my fault that I lost the baby. While he was talking, I thought about the dream I had.

I just came to tell you that I'm taking my sister with me. She's sick, Mommy, and it'll hurt less if she comes with me now."

"What do you mean take your sister with you? I don't have a daughter. You were my only baby."

"I have to go, just know we love you. We will continue to watch over you and daddy."

"Ms. Summers?" the doctor called out to me, breaking my thoughts.

"Yes?"

He looked over at my uncle. I knew he wanted to know if it was okay for him to speak in front of them.

"Well, we will get going. Justice, Neen, call us if you need anything," Latrell said.

Once they left, the doctor continued.

"Ms. Summers, there was absolutely nothing you could have done to prevent this from happening. It's one of those things that just happens for a reason. You didn't do anything wrong. I know it's a hard situation to deal with, but it looks like you have a great support system," Dr. Dell stated. He gave me a prescription and sent me on my way.

We were finally home and my mom was waiting on me hand and foot. She asked E would it be okay for her to stay and look after me. She didn't want to seem like she was overstepping her boundaries. But he liked the fact that she was around and helping us out, especially around the house. All I wanted to do was lay down. I didn't feel like talking or discussing what happened to anyone, which is why I told E not to tell the crew right away, I just needed time alone.

E helped me shower and change into my pajamas. He lotioned me down and then massaged my back before I drifted off to sleep with tears in my eyes. Losing one child is a lot to deal with, but to lose another one that you were looking forward to raising to fill that void in your heart was the worst feeling ever.

LOVONNA

J knew I shouldn't have eaten that seafood. Von had taken Volante and I out for dinner at a seafood restaurant. I was never one that could eat seafood, it always messed with stomach. At that moment, I was on the toilet shitting out my insides.

"Damn, what the fuck is that smell?" Von asked, coming into the bathroom.

"Von! Get out!"

"Damn, that's you in here? I thought it was a sewer or some shit. Damn, lil' baby, you need to drop one, flush one. That shit coming through the vents," he indicated.

"It's the seafood. I'm not really supposed to eat it because it always makes me sick."

"Man, I love your ass, but please don't eat that shit again. Lil' shitty booty ass, make sure you bathe after that."

He was laughing and I just stared at him as shit continued to run out of my ass. I was slightly embarrassed, but I didn't have time to focus on that.

"Trigga, get the fuck out!"

"Don't get mad at me because you ate something you weren't supposed to eat."

"Get out now!" I yelled.

He turned around to walk away, but I heard him mumble something else and then laughed about it. His ass strolled back into the bathroom and lit a candle.

"There, because you got my walls screaming for help."

I rolled my eyes to show how irritated I really was at him. I didn't have a problem with using the restroom around him but damn, some privacy should be given.

After I soaked in the tub for what seemed like for hours, I made my way down to the living room.

"I hope you washed your ass good," Von said.

"Stop cursing in front of him," I told him, ignoring his comment.

"Damn, you right. I mean, yeah, you're right."

I sat down, and he licked his lips at me. I wasn't even in the mood, since my stomach was still hurting. We watched a movie until Volante fell asleep and Von went to put him to bed. I stared at them and smiled. He was a great father, he could have easily abandoned Volante like some men do their children. But he stepped up and did what he needed to do.

"I have something for you," Von mentioned as he sat next to me. He held a small bag up. I grabbed it and looked inside. I opened the box and saw a charm bracelet with a stethoscope, a lab coat, and a mask charm.

"I love this, Von, when did you get this?" I asked.

"In the Bahamas. When I noticed those charms, I knew I had to get it from you."

"Thank you, baby."

Kissing his lips, I wanted to show him how thankful I was, but I didn't know if my stomach would be okay with it. Being that Von's dick was so damn big, I knew he would be in my stomach.

"Let me slide up in that real quick before I leave."

"Where are you going?" I asked.

"Lo, I told you I had some business to handle later, remember?"

"Oh, yeah. I just forgot."

"Do you have a problem with watching Volante?"

"No, I just forgot, and why would I have a problem with that?"

"I'm just making sure. I know he's not yours."

"It's cool, Von, and he's asleep anyway."

"I won't be out too late, lil' baby."

"I'm not worried. I'll probably be asleep anyway," I told him.

"You look magically delicious in them boy shorts, you know that?" he asked.

I giggled so hard because when he wanted some, he wouldn't stop until he got it. I decided to ignore my bubbling stomach. I straddled his lap, and he immediately put a finger inside of my juice box.

"You so damn wet and tight. I can't stop fucking you if I wanted to."

I got up to take my shorts off, and he had my lil' friend or should I say big friend, waiting. He was still sitting on the couch, so I got on top of him so that I could take a ride into the night that would put me in a coma.

It was late into the night when I heard Volante crying. I quickly got up to see what the matter was. Von still hadn't made it home, and I was sure to curse his ass out. I gently pushed the door open to Volante's room.

"Volante, what's wrong?"

"I want my daddy."

"He'll be here shortly. do you want something to drink?"

"No, I want my daddy."

I walked away and called Von. When he answered, I went in on him about being out later than he said he would be. I told him that Volante wanted him. He told me to put him on speaker and go into his room.

"Hey, son, daddy is on his way. If you need anything, Ms. Vonna can help you."

"No, Mommy said she can't," Volante stated.

"Mommy said Vonna can't what?" Von questioned. I should had known her ass had put a bug in the child's ear. Typical baby mama.

"That she can't tell me what to do or she can't touch me."

I heard the sigh coming from Von. He told Volante he could trust me and that I was only trying to help him. Once Volante seemed to have calmed down, I left his room.

"I'm going to fuck that hoe up. Why the fuck would she tell a child that shit?" he asked.

"I don't know, Von, are you really on your way?"

"Give me another hour, lil' baby, and I'll be there. I'm handling some important business right now."

I hung up on him. I knew what type of business he had going on, but I felt like he should have been home with me and his child. I wasn't looking forward to all the late nights. It didn't bother me when I was away at school.

LAVONDRIUS

"Okay, so what the fuck you saying?" I asked my private investigator. We had him check Nivea out. I had been gone from home longer than what I expected, but we had to figure some shit out. I wasn't going to lay my head down without some fucking answers.

"What I'm saying is, Nivea has no connections with your father from what I can find."

"Well, how the fuck she found out some personal information about me?" Diggy asked him.

"Look, I know you guys want answers, but this is going to take more than one day to figure out. I'll have to be on her for at least two weeks to a month. Depending on what all she does, it could be sooner," Saver stated.

We gave him that name a long time ago because in a way, he is a saver.

"Aight, you know I hate resting my head when I can't figure shit out," I told him.

"Let me do my job. I promise I'll have something for you guys."

He left, and I talked with Diggy about the situation more. My phone rang, and it was Lo. I answered it, and she went in on a nigga.

Diggy was dying laughing while sitting next to me. I wanted to punch his ass.

After calming her and Volante down, I told Lo I would be home in about an hour. I continued talking with Diggy about some shit.

"You know Risa moving in with me in a few weeks?" he asked me.

"Yeah, Lo told me.

"So, what y'all on?"

"You already know how I feel about lil' baby. That's my heart. I ain't have this much love for Layla ass."

"Yo, when I first met them, I knew you would love her ass."

"You already know how I do. Just trying to decide what we gon' do. She wants to stay there for her residency. I have to be accessible for Volante. I'm just going with the flow right now."

"Y'all gon' be straight, but what's up with E and Neen?"

My phone started to ring before I could even respond to his question. It was Saver and something told me that I wouldn't like what would be discussed on the call. I put it on speaker so that Diggy could hear.

"Speak, I told him.

"I got someone watching Nivea, but something told me to hunt down your father as well. I spotted him leaving the bar with Layla. I talked with old man Dingy there, and he let me view footage of the bar. They did a lot of drinking, which could explain how friendly and close they were to one another. Anyway, he walked her to her car and looked at her as if she was the most beautiful person in the world to him. They didn't kiss or hug, she just got into her car and left. But, hear this, while I was watching them, your mom was as well."

"You kidding me, right?"

"I wish, she pulled up on your dad and started going off on him. He took a few blows to the head. Your mom got a mean left hook."

"Don't I know it, so what happened after that?"

"Police was called, but your mom left before they got there. Your dad did as well."

"Anything else?" I asked him.

"Nope, I'll be in touch."

I looked over at Diggy.

"Layla and my dad, huh?"

"I can't wait for the outcome of this," he mentioned.

Walking into my house, I tried to be as quiet as possible. It seemed like the more careful I was, the more shit I bumped into. Next thing I know, Lo was standing at the top of the staircase looking down at me. A nigga didn't know if he should go up or stay down.

"Is it safe to come up?" I asked.

"Come find out."

I slowly walked up the steps. I knew I was pissing her off even more by walking so slow. When I made it up, I walked slowly by her. She reached out to grab me, but I quickly jumped away.

"Trigga, don't play with me."

"Shit, I thought you was about to lay hands on a nigga."

She followed me into the room, and I couldn't deal with the silence. I turned around and kissed her.

"You been drinking?" she asked.

"Yes, momma, I have."

"Go shower, and you smell like weed."

"Damn, it didn't bother you before. What's up?"

"Nothing."

"Nah, we been in this shit long enough. Tell me what the problem is."

"First off, you tell me you won't be gone long. Volante started screaming, and I couldn't even calm him down because he was told that I can't tell him what to do, or touch him. What type of shit is that bitch on? I didn't do shit to her. I'm not about to deal with this drama shit, I got too much going on to be involved with all of this."

"Damn, straight like that. That's what you gon' say?"

"Trigga, look, no matter what we say or do, this shit gon' be hard. I can already tell. I'm trying to ride this out with you, but at what cost? I have goals and dreams, and this wasn't what I bargained for. I love you, and I have no problem with Volante, but I can't deal with all that drama. If his mother is going to continue to poison his mind, I rather just step away."

I really didn't know how to take the shit that she was spitting at me. I get that she was focused on school, but the way she said the shit made me think she wanted us to end.

"So, what are you saying, LoVonna?"

"Von, look at me and tell me that this isn't already stressful. I'm twenty years old. I'm not ready for all of this yet. I love you, but I love myself more. I want to be successful, I can't do that with all of the drama that is coming. Believe me, I know it is, you're going to go in on Layla about what Volante said, and she's going to come at you with more shit. Because I'm with you, she's going to try to make your life hell. Why would you even want that?"

"I really don't know what to say to you right now. I get that you're this strong woman, and you want to remain focused, but how you think that makes me feel. We have to compromise, LoVonna, if we're going to make this work.—"

"Compromise? Trigga—"

"Why the fuck is you calling me that!" I yelled. She only called me Trigga when her ass was mad or if I was fucking her good. In the moment wasn't no *fucking* going on.

"Look, I love you, but—"

"I'm not really into hearing no buts, if you want to leave, Lo, you know where the door is at."

"Von, it's not even like that. I'm just trying to get you to understand."

"I understand. Your education is more important. I'm good with that."

"Von, don't make it seem like I'm choosing."

"You are, but like I said. I'm good with that."

"Good with what?"

"With you wanting to end things. Ain't that basically what you're getting at?" I asked her.

When she didn't respond, I knew the answer. I left her there with her own fucked up thoughts. I showered and washed away the day's burdens. If only it was that easy to do, right?

Drying off, I made my way back into the room. I didn't even

bother to put lotion on. Lo was already laying down in the bed. Her eyes were on the ceiling.

Am I being selfish? I thought to myself. I didn't want what we had to end, but my son came first. Once I got into the bed, Lo looked over at me. I looked into her eyes and tears immediately started to fall. I knew it was over. At that moment, I knew I was being selfish. Her life shouldn't be tarnished with my baggage.

Pulling her closer to me, I held her close. I couldn't predict what the future held for us, but I damn sure didn't think losing her would be a factor.

It was early morning, and I was in the kitchen making breakfast. Lo was still asleep, so I eased out of the bed so that I wouldn't wake her. Volante sat in the living room waiting for me to finish breakfast. I had a long talk with him about his mother and the shit that she told him. Let's just say, he won't be repeating shit else his mother tells him.

Volante sat at the table eating away. I ate my omelet while watching him go in on his pancakes. I felt a presence so I turned around and noticed Lo staring at us.

"Good morning," I told her.

"Hey."

"Good morning, Ms. Vonna," Volante said.

"Good morning, Volante."

"You hungry?" I asked her.

"Nah, I'm good. We're hitting the highway in a bit."

"Okay, you need anything?" I asked.

"Nah, do you?"

"Yeah, I do," I told her.

"What?"

"You."

She looked down at her hands. I don't know why my heart skipped a beat, but it did.

"When you're done, let me know, I'll clean the kitchen," she said.

My eyes glanced over her and saw that she was wearing some shorts and a crop top. Her hair was in a messy bun on the top of her head. *She's the one*, I thought.

"Finish eating," I told Volante. I got up and walked up to Lo. I gently pushed her toward the living room area.

"So, what's up, you leaving a nigga?"

"Von, I never said that."

"And you didn't say you weren't either. Look, I know I have a lot of baggage. I wish I could change the shit, but I can't. I love you, but if you feel my life is too much for yours, I'll happily let you go, no feelings lost.

"I'm not saying that I don't want to be with you, Von."

"Then, what the fuck are you saying?"

"I don't know. I just don't won't to lose sight of what's most important."

"Well, sorry if I fucking didn't get the memo because I thought I was important to you!"

"Von?"

I walked away because the shit was getting old by the minute. I continued to eat with my son. After we finished, I cleaned the kitchen and took him to the park. I told Lo I was taking him, and she just said okay. She was packing her things to leave, and I was ready for her ass to go.

Elijah

I was making dinner for Neen and me when she came into the kitchen. I hadn't seen her smile in a few weeks. We prayed together, and we visited lil' EJ's grave every day, sometimes twice a day.

"Hey, what are you doing?" she asked me.

"Making dinner for us."

"Wow, you haven't cook for me in a long time."

"I know, that's because you be throwing down in the kitchen."

"Whatever," she said, smiling. I just stared at her. That smile did something to me. I knew what I had to do, and the timing was just right.

"Neen, you are so beautiful."

With that, I left to get what I needed. Once I returned, she was still standing in the same spot, looking at her phone.

"Neen, we been through a lot together. I couldn't imagine going through everything we been through with anyone else, but you," I said, dropping down on one knee. "Neen Summers, will you marry me?"

She glanced at the ring and placed her hand on her chest. Tears flew down her eyes, and she tried to talk, but nothing came out. Eventually, she got it out.

"You want to marry me even though I can't give you a child?" she asked.

"I want to marry you because you've given me so much more. Neen, maybe God wants our family to be a union before we have child. I'm ready for that, I'm ready for God to be involved in our lives. I know I'm not a saint, but he created you just for me, and I'm claiming what's mine, so again I ask, Neen Summers, will you marry me?"

"Yes, Elijah, I will marry you."

I got up from my knee and kissed her. I held her tight and whispered into her ear.

"I want to marry you tomorrow."

"Tomorrow?"

"Yes, tomorrow. Your mom will be there. She knew I was going to propose. If you want the crew there as well, I'll make it happen."

"Yes, E, I want them there. I'll marry you tomorrow, baby."

She was jumping up and down with the biggest grin on her face.

After hugging and kissing, we had called everyone and told them the good news. Risa and Vonna were on the highway, but they said they were turning around to head back. I knew they had class, but they knew how important the moment was for us. I called up the designers and a few other people to help make our day special.

Standing next to Neen at the courthouse, I admired how beautiful she looked. Trigga made the designer design her a nice dress overnight. My baby was looking so beautiful. I just decided on a pair of slacks and a nice button up shirt. We got to exchange vows even though it wasn't that type of a wedding. Our witnesses stepped forward to sign. I had Trigga sign for me and Neen had Risa sign as her witness.

"Oh my God, I can't believe you two are married!" Risa yelled.

We all got into our cars to head over to my crib. We wanted a more private intimate dinner, so we had it catered at my home. I don't know what was going on with Trigga and Vonna, but the shit was obvious. She drove her car, while he drove his. I even heard she stayed at her parents after turning around to come back after I called them.

While the helpers set up for dinner, the guys and I decided we needed to smoke something. We headed to the side of the house away from the women. The canopy was big with lights shining all over. It damn sure wasn't what I had in mind, but it exceeded my expectations being that it was last minute.

"Man, you finally did it. You finally got married," Trigga stated.

"I know, y'all remember when I first asked her ass to marry me, she took off running. She really thought I was playing, but a nigga was dead ass. Even though I had just met her that day."

"Nigga, your ass was hurt for real. But aye, your wish came true," Diggy stated.

"I love Neen with everything in me. I would give that girl the world. I know I did my dirt, but I would never do that shit again. Especially now that I'm married. I know I told y'all to not bring up the baby thing around her, but I think talking about it helps. At least for me it does. I think Neen feels less of a woman for some reason, but I'll continue to shower her with love. Even if we don't have a child, we will always be good," I revealed.

"I know, I had to keep telling Risa to not say anything, not sure if she did or not," Diggy spoke as he passed the blunt to Trigga.

"The food is here. Oh, and Diggy, Risa's father and mother are here too," Lo said.

"Like hell! I know he ain't showing his face after the shit he did!" Diggy stood.

145

"Diggy, don't make shit worse than it already is," Trigga told him.

"The only reason I'll be on chill is because this is Neen's day," he told me.

Vonna stood there looking back and forth between us. I walked off with Diggy beside me. Trigga was puffin' on the last of that good shit.

"Let me try it," I heard Vonna say.

"Hell nah."

"Von, please."

"Nah, I haven't talked to your ass since I left to take my son to the park, and the first thing you say to me is something about trying this good good?"

Diggy and I stopped and turned around. We didn't even know they were having issues.

"Von, can we talk later?"

"I'm straight, LoVonna. I'm sure you got more important things to be worrying about."

Vonna turned around and walked away. She damn near knocked Diggy ass over when she walked by him.

"Damn, sis, you good?" he asked.

She didn't respond, she just kept going. I looked over at Trigg, and he had that nonchalant look on his face.

"I'm ready to eat," he told us, walking off.

Inside the house stood Risa's parents. I could tell she wasn't that happy for them to be there.

"Congratulations, young man, you've made an honest woman of Neen. I give you my dearest respect," Larell stated.

"Thank you, sir," I told him.

I walked off to find my wife. When I saw her, she was feeding her face. I was happy because she finally got her appetite back.

"I hope you save some for everyone else."

"I'll always save my husband some food. The King eats first."

She had a nigga cheesing.

"I like when you call me your husband."

I walked over to her and pulled her up from the chair she was occupying and kissed her.

"Thank you, Neen."

"For what?" she questioned me.

"Thank you for being everything I needed you to be."

"Aww, don't make me cry."

"I'm serious, lil' baby. You really cuffed a nigga for life. I know you dreamed of a big beautiful wedding, but I dreamed of having you with or without a wedding. I know I hurt you before, and I am sincerely sorry, Mrs. Stokes. I know you said I have given you the world already, but I want to give you so much more. Whatever you want, I got you."

"Mr. Stokes, you're all that I need."

"Okay, enough of that shit, can we eat now?" Trigga asked, walking into the canopy.

As everyone sat down, we finally ate.

Clink. Clink.

That was Justice trying to get everyone's attention. She used her fork to clink against the champagne glass.

"I want to make an announcement," she said.

Everyone stopped eating and gave her their undivided attention.

"I just want to say a few words to you two. I know you two both had a few ups and downs but with your continuous faith in the Lord, you pulled through. Elijah, I know you don't liked to be called by your real name, but I just want to say thank you for taking care of my child's heart. There are so many things I could say, but that is all that matters. God makes no mistakes, I just want you two to know that. The future holds many possibilities. Don't rush God's plan, be patient with him. I love you two so much, and your angels are smiling down at you."

She sat down because she had started crying. Neen wiped her tears that fell. I pulled her close and watched Latrell walk over to Justice. He comforted her and asked what she meant about angels. She explained that we lost two children. Everyone took turns saying a few things with well wishes for us. I thought about what Neen's mother said to us about the future. One thing I knew was, I wasn't going to put my wife through that pain again, no matter how bad I wanted a son because it wasn't fair to her. If she didn't want to try again, I wasn't going to press the issue.

After dinner, we sat around just chatting and listening to Justice and Larell tell embarrassing stories about Neen as a child. For him to be distant in her adult life, he sure had a lot of stories to tell.

"Well, we're going to get out of here. Von and I have to get going," Risa told us.

"Thank you both for coming, it meant a lot to us," I told them.

Neen got up to hug them and I did as well.

"Larisa, can your mother and I talk with you for a moment?" Larell asked Risa.

It wasn't like everyone didn't know what the fuck he did. We all just wanted to know what Risa's answer would be.

LARISA

*I*t's been a while since I talked or seen my father. I was kind of upset that he had shown up without even talking to me about it, but it wasn't about me, it was about Neen. While everyone chatted and talked after dinner, he tried to laugh at my jokes. It was really pissing me off, but Darcel told me to stop acting like I hated him. If only he knew, but I know Darcel wants me to forgive my father. His parents died, and he would give anything to have them back.

"Larisa, can your mother and I talk with you for a moment?" my dad asked me.

"Sure."

I excused myself, and they did as well. They hugged Neen on the way out. We walked around the back and sat on the sectional set they had outdoors. It was very nice and comfy. My mother sat down, and I searched around for my father.

"He's coming. I just wanted to talk to you while he grabs Darcel."

"Why is he bringing Darcel out?"

"You'll see, but first, I just want to apologize for not being there for you. I know how you feel about Darcel. I see the look in your eyes. I guess I should be happy because I honestly thought you were going to be gay."

"Gay? Why would you think that, Mother?"

"I mean, you never really dated or talked to any guys at your school. I never even caught you talking on the phone to a guy. But seeing you happy should have been most important."

I smiled because even though I was still mad at her and my father, I knew she was just being an overprotective mother. Before I could respond, Darcel and my father came walking up. My mom gestured for Darcel to sit next to her, and he did. He looked over at me and winked. My father sat next to me, directly across from Darcel.

"I first want to apologize to you both. What I did was over the top, but what I won't apologize for, is being a father that loves his daughter. Larisa, baby, I love you more than life itself. I know what I did was wrong, but all I wanted to do was protect you and your future. You're all grown up now, so I guess I have to let you go."

"Sir, you don't have to let her go. She's always going to be your daughter. Only difference is, she now has two men in her life that will protect her. I respect what you did as a father because one day when I'm married, have children and God gives me a girl, I'll be the same way. I just hope and pray she finds someone that'll respect and care for her as I do for Risa. I don't have a motive to hurt her. I love her. I'm not distracting her from her classes because she knows I don't applaud anything less than a 'B', and I help her when she needs it, and push her to go harder. She's smart, beautiful, and strong-headed. You've talked to Saliburry, so you know all about me, but never will I put Larisa in harm's way. I'm legit. Yes, I have my hands in some-things, but I'm smart and know when and what I should be doing. Is it ideal? No, but my empire is solid."

"Darcel, call me Larell. I see the way you look at my daughter. It's the same way I look at her mother. I'll admit, your side hustle still bothers me, but Saliburry did say your operations are tight. The only reason he told me about you was because he's been in our family since Risa was a baby. He knows how I feel about my daughter. I won't stand in the way of your happiness. Just don't bring any harm or danger to my child. Because if you do, then Mr. Darcel, we gon' have a major problem. One that your lil' crew won't be able to handle."

My eyes bucked, and I looked at Darcel who didn't seemed moved at all. I was fucking with a real King and to know I cuffed him, had me smiling. Once Darcel responded, I decided to speak since I didn't get a word in.

"Dad, Darcel wanted me to reach out to you and mom, but I was so mad at you both. I just couldn't understand why my parents, who say they love me so much, could pull some mess like that."

"I know, and I am embarrassed by it. I'm sorry, Risa, please forgive me," he said.

I looked at my father and admired how handsome he really was. Even the gray hairs looked good on him.

"I forgive you," I told him.

"I don't care to know if you two are having sex, which, I already know the answer to because Risa has gotten thick. Only good penis does that to you," my mom pointed out.

"Mom!" I yelled while shaking my head. That was so inappropriate and embarrassing.

"Lanetta, I don't want to hear nothing about penis and my daughter in the same sentence."

My father got up and walked away quickly. My mom looked at us and smiled.

"Well, you two are grown. Just tell me is it good?" she asked.

My eyes grew so big, and I knew my cheeks had to have been red. I knew she had had one too many glasses of wine.

"It's most definitely good, Ma," Darcel told her.

"Darcel, don't. I can't take you two, I'm out."

I walked away, and I heard them still talking.

"Well, I see why she's so gone over you," she told him.

"She got me whipped too, Ma," he responded back.

Instead of walking, I ran so I couldn't hear shit else they had to say. Who just wants to know about their daughter's sex life? And what boyfriend tells their girl's mom about their sex life? I knew my mom was a freak because she had my father making some strange noises. I used to just put my headphones on and listen to my music when they had sex. Ugh, just thinking about it made me want to vomit.

My parents had left and Darcel had me against Vonna's car, tonguing me down. She and Trigga walked off somewhere talking.

"I can kiss your ass all day. I never used to like kissing," he told me.

"I have that effect on men. I won best kisser in high school."

I giggled so hard because he looked like he wanted to kill me.

"Don't play with me. Those lips had better only been on me."

"I'm just playing with you."

"Anyway, I told your moms you were moving in with me."

I grabbed the bottle water I had on the hood of the car and took a few sips.

"Why? What did she say?" I asked, taking another few sips of water.

"Because I felt she needed to know, and she didn't say shit, only that I would have in-house pussy whenever I wanted."

I had spit my water all over his shirt, arm, and neck when he said that shit. It was going to be awhile before I brought them around each other again. She went from supporting my father not wanting us together to talking about us sexing each other.

"Girl, I know damn well you ain't spit water on me. You better find something and clean me up."

He was so damn pissed at me. It was a good thing I had wipes inside of my bag in the car. I got out a few and wiped him down. He mean mugged me the whole time.

"You ready, Risa?" Vonna asked. She didn't look very happy, so I kissed Darcel with his mean ass and hopped into the car.

Three weeks later...

LAVONDRIUS

"Saver, you been blowing me up all day. I hope you got some information on Nivea," I told him.

"Is Diggy and E with you? And how long have you known LoVonna?" he asked.

"Yeah, you do know we had a meeting today, and about nine going on ten months now, why?"

"Okay, Trigga. The information I have is for your ears to hear first. After that, you can tell whoever. I just wanted to know about the timeframe of your relationship that's all."

"Where you at?" I asked.

"My spot."

"Be there in twenty, I'm about to bail out now."

He hung up, and I told Diggy and E that I had to meet with Saver.

"Fuck you mean meet? That shit sounds suspicious. You know damn well we ain't letting you go alone," E stated and Diggy agreed.

"Look, I think it's info on my father. I'll be straight. They don't call me Trigga for nothing."

"I don't know, the fact that Tommy is still living, he's making that name go down in shame," Diggy expressed.

"I'm out. Oh, and by the way. Tommy is dead, he been dead about two months now," I told them.

"Dead? Why the fuck we ain't get the memo? Who killed him?" E asked.

I chuckled and proceeded to leave. But they weren't having that.

"Hell fucking nah, I know damn well you ain't off that nigga and didn't say shit to us. We better than that," Diggy spoke.

"Just living up to my name, don't want it to go down in shame. Besides, I like doing shit in silence. I wanted him to think shit was all good. Once he got comfortable, I made my move."

"Well I'll be damned. But we got eyes on you. I still don't like that you're going to meet up with Saver alone," E argued.

"If it'll make y'all feel better, y'all can follow behind."

Walking into Saver's apartment after he let me in, he locked the doors behind me. Nigga had six locks.

"Saver, the amount of money we pay you, I know you can afford a crib of your own. Why the hell you living in this small ass apartment?"

"It's only temporarily. My home is being built. You know the line of work I'm in. I have to make sure my home is secured. I can't live in a home that's already designed and that way, I can hide cameras within my walls."

"You know you sound like a pervert, right?"

"Never will I be that. Unless I see a fine honey with a fat ass. I pay these chicks no mind. Besides, I am married remember?"

"Damn, I forgot all about you being married. Tell me the story of why she can't live with you again?"

"Her son hates me. So, until he accepts me, she'll continue to live in Arizona while I'm here catching blue balls."

"Saver, listen to me when I tell you this, wife or no wife, in your situation, you're liable to go out there and fuck the first woman you see."

We laughed and got down to business. He showed me pictures. The first picture was Nivea and the second picture was of a nigga. The same nigga I saw on the boat that looked damn near identical to me.

"What the fuck is this?" I asked.

154

"Trigga, you know I have mad love for you, but when I tell you this, I need you to keep a leveled head. You're going to need it to strategize your next move. I'm glad your crew came along even though I told you to come alone, but they may need to help you walk out of here."

"The fuck you mean?" I pulled my gun from my waist.

"Trigga, it's nothing like that and besides, I have no reason to set you up. I just know the news I'm about to deliver will be knee-buckling."

"Just say the shit," I told him, putting my gun away.

"You already know the girl in the picture, but the guy… that's your brother, your older brother."

"Come again?"

"His name is Volante Jr. He's thirty-four years old. His mother is Tina White. Your father cheated on your mother with her. The story is, your mother wanted nothing to do with the child. Your dad abandoned him and now Volante Jr. wants revenge. He also was in the Bahamas the exact same time you and your crew were. Nivea was brought in as a diversion. She was brought in to get in good with Diggy. Diggy being the guy that he is didn't take the bait. I'm not sure what else they have in the works, but it's not good. However, I can't seem to find out how he got so much info on you and your crew. It couldn't have been your father."

"Un-fucking believable! That nigga stood face-to-face with me. I'm always on my A-game, but being that we didn't take no heat on the boat with us, he had the upper-hand. My father just abandoned him and now he's what, out to get him and me?"

"It looks that way because why would he bring Nivea in to get at Diggy? He knew you were going to the Bahamas. Something isn't adding up. If your father doesn't know about him, someone in your crew does, and they're helping him."

"My crew too solid. I know that for a fact. Tommy was on the other end, so I knew what type of nigga he was from the start."

"I brought in some help on this one. I'll have eyes on Volante Jr. 24/7," he told me.

"This shit is crazy, my son is named after my father, and he already has a fucking junior."

"Speaking of your father, he's been spending a lot of time at Layla's place. Not to get into your business, but do you think it's a possibility that your son is really your brother?"

"Trust me, I thought about the shut, but he's mine. DNA don't lie."

"When you got tested was it at a place she chose?" he asked.

"Yeah, why?"

"Just asking; people do some grimy shit."

"So, you think my dad and Layla are fraud?"

"I wouldn't put it past them," he voiced.

"I don't even know what I should do with the information you gave. I have a brother? My parents hid the shit from me, but for what? Because my mom didn't accept him?"

"I'm sorry I had to be the one to tell you."

"It's all good, it's going to take time to process all of this shit, and how the hell did you know that my crew tagged along?"

"Because I know them."

We chuckled and talked about the shit a bit more. I told him the money would be in his account in a few hours. I left and met up with Diggy and E. Since Diggy's house was the closest, we decided on his crib. Sitting on his couch, we passed around a few blunts before I finally was able to tell them all the shit Saver had told me.

"I think I'm hearing shit. You got an older brother?" Diggy asked.

"Man, same shit I said," I voiced to him.

"So, what now?" E asked.

"Saver got someone watching him. But he must have eyes on us. Who all knew about the Bahamas trip, besides the members in our crew?"

"Shit, nobody, you know our team loyal," E stated.

"Layla knew, but it seems as if she spends her time with my father."

"That ain't a good look, what type of shit he on?" E asked.

"We shall find out. Just have to wait this shit out," I pointed out.

"What's up with you and Vonna? I'm going to get Risa next week and we'll bring her things back. She's going to drive her car back, y'all know my baby hate the highway."

"You getting a U-Haul?"

"Yeah, why you want to roll with me? Matter of fact your ass can drive the U-Haul back."

"Nigga, what the fuck I look like. Ain't no reason for me to go anyway."

"So, again I ask… what's up with you and Vonna?"

"He heard you the first time, he just didn't want to answer. Apparently, Vonna focusing on school, she ain't ready for the whole step momma shit," E stated.

"Man, shut up, that's why I don't tell your ass shit. Got shit all twisted up," I defined.

"Well tell me, shit, because I'm confused as hell," Diggy stated.

"To be honest, I don't know. I'm not worried about it either. She wanna focus on school, I got baggage, and it ain't fair to her."

"Baggage? Volante?" he asked.

"Yep, Layla had put some shit in his ear and he repeated it. Lo been in her feelings ever since."

"Damn, yeah, that shit will make a real one detour, but she knew what it was because y'all talked about the shit."

"I'm good on her, and we talk here and there. Well she do, I just sit on the phone and listen to her ask the same question over and over."

"And what question is that?" Diggy asked.

"Do I still love her?"

"Nigga, and what the fuck you be saying?"

"Y'all acting like some straight bitches. But it ain't really like that, she calls here and there just to say she still loves a nigga. She'll ask if I still love her. I tell her I do and we get off the phone. I miss my lil' baby, but shit, y'all know Trigga don't chase 'em, he replace him."

"Yeah, okay, how come you haven't replaced her yet?" E asked.

"I got other shit to worry about, matter of fact, let me get up out of here before the storm hits."

"Damn, I forgot that storm coming through tonight, let me get my ass home. Neen scary ass hate when I'm away when it storms."

E and I left to head home. I told Diggy I would hit him up later. I felt a drip of rain hit my skin and I knew the rain was due. Once I got in the car, my phone sounded off. It was Lo calling me on FaceTime.

"What up?" I asked her.

"Nothing, just sitting around staring at all of Risa's boxes. I can't believe she's leaving me."

"You already know she's going to call you every day and every hour."

"Don't I know it? I'm just going to miss her."

"She wants to be with her man. Can't fault her for that."

"I'm not. Anyway, where are you going? I see you sitting in your car."

"I'm was heading home."

"From?"

"Diggy's."

"Oh, well you can hit me back when you get in. It's raining so hard here."

"Yeah, it about to start raining in minute here as well. But, I'll hit you when I make it in."

"Okay."

I ended the call before she could say more. I wished shit was the same between us, but she made the decision for me. After the argument we had a few weeks ago about her needing to focus on school, I fell back. We only talk when she called because I damn sure wasn't going to call her after the shit she said to me.

Once I made it into the house, it started pouring down raining.

"You made it just in time," Truth told me.

"Man, who you telling. Where Baby at?"

"In the back. I just fed her. I think she misses Vonna. She hasn't been herself coming over here."

"I noticed that. Well she's going to have to get used to not seeing her around."

"She's still focusing on school?"

"You sound like me?"

"You say it to be sarcastic, I'm asking because I know it won't last

158

long. That girl thinks about you night and day. She's just afraid of drama coming into her life. You can't blame the girl for wanting to be something in life."

"I don't blame her, but to make it seem like I don't mean shit to her. It is what it is though."

"You're so in love, you don't know what to do."

"I can't even sit up here and lie because I do love her ass, but she making a nigga feel weak."

"Showing your feelings don't make you weak. It makes you a man. Just continue to answer her calls, and call the girl once in a while. She's going to start thinking you don't care about her."

"I wonder why I can't get this same conversation from my damn mother."

"We've been down this road before, Trigga, she's not that type of woman. I honestly don't know why she even had a damn child."

"Probably because her husband had a son, so she wanted one too."

"What?" Truth asked.

"My father has a son... other than me. He's thirty-four years old." Truth knew I didn't lie about shit like that. She sat down on the couch, staring at me.

"I couldn't believe it either."

"Let me guess, Saver?" she asked.

"You know it."

"Wow, I'm so sorry you got stuck with those parents. But you know I love you like you're my own."

"I know, Truth, and I thank you for showing me unconditional love and for always putting me in my place."

"I'm going to leave this conversation alone because I already know you have something plotting. Just be careful."

"You staying here tonight?" I asked.

"Yeah, why? You got someone coming over?"

"I just might," I said, walking away.

"Yeah right. Baby gon' tear their ankles up."

I laughed all the way up to my room. I called for Baby, but she never came. She was really missing Lo. I showered and decided to FaceTime her back.

"Hey, didn't think you would hit me back," she stated.

"I wasn't going to, but Baby missing you. She won't even come upstairs."

"Aww, I miss her too."

"So, what's been up?"

"Nothing really... the semester ends next week. I already studied my life away, so I'm just taking a break before I overload my brain."

"You got a big ass head, so you got more room to store a few more things."

"Not funny."

"I miss your sexy ass, lil' baby."

"Do you? Because lately it hasn't been seeming like it."

"Been handling a lot of shit, that's all."

"What's wrong?" she asked.

Usually when one of us asked that question, we would spill our hearts out.

"It ain't shit."

"Tell me, I mean I know things are different, but that doesn't change how I feel about you."

"Just tell me what is it that we're doing?" I asked.

"I keep asking myself that question, and I know I don't want to live my life without you. It's just hard you know. I'm trying to be all that I can, but... I don't know."

"But your ideal man has a child, right?"

"It's not that, Von, it's the drama that comes with it."

"Lil' baby, I promise you that you'll never have to worry about that. On some real shit, I need you. I'm going through some shit right now. I'm the man in these streets and I can handle anything my way, but just knowing your woman is there for you does something to a nigga soul."

"I'm here, Von," she stated as a tear rolled down her eyes.

"Why you crying?"

"Because, I'm realizing how selfish I'm being. I'm sorry."

"It's all good, baby. The ambition in you will allow you to succeed and will get you far. I'm gon' always be here for you regardless."

"I love you."

"I love you more."

"I wanted to surprise you with the news, but I'll tell you now so that'll probably brighten up your day," she expressed.

"You're pregnant?" I asked.

"What? No, why is that the first thing black people ask when someone tells them they got some news to share?"

"My fault, that's what came to my mind. So, what is it?"

"I've decided to do my residency back home."

"Word? When were you planning on telling me?"

"I guess when I moved back next week."

"So, you're moving out too?"

"Yeah, it's too big for me anyway. I already found a two-bedroom condo that I like."

"Damn, you've done a lot. Why didn't you ask to stay with me?"

"I... I don't know. That's not something you ask. That's like me asking for your hand in marriage."

"Nah, that's not."

"I'm saying it's something a woman shouldn't do. What if you weren't ready for all of that, and I asked you?"

"You know how I feel about you, Lo, I want you to come stay with me, lil' baby."

She looked down, and I knew she had her doubts.

"What, you're not ready?" I asked.

"It's not that, I mean. Yes, Von, I will stay with you."

"You sure?"

"Positive."

"Why?"

"Why what?"

"Why you want to stay with me?"

"I want to wake up to you every day. Von, you're my world, and all I know is you. My life doesn't make sense without you in it. But I have to tell you something before I move in."

"Tell me."

"I can't over the phone. I think its best face-to-face,"

"Aight. So, what day we moving your stuff?"

"Next Thursday, but Diggy is helping Risa, so he said he'll help me as well."

"Nah, I got you. What all you bringing? And that nigga always withholding information from my ass."

"I was going to put everything in storage until I got my condo, but you have a bed and furniture. I don't know where I'm going to put it."

"You know that room in the basement?

"Yeah."

"You can put it there. I been wanting to fix that up into a room."

"You sure?"

I heard a loud noise coming from her background, and it sounded like screams.

"What the fuck was that?" I asked. I saw the panic look on her face. She got up, and I heard her yelling out to Risa. It got really quiet. I called out Lo's name but got no response. Then it happened. He showed his face, it was my father's so-called son on the other end of the phone looking at me.

"You know, I was jealous at the fact that you have our father all to yourself, but seeing that you got this sexy ass woman makes me hate you even more."

And just like that the video ended. My phone rang, and it was Saver.

"Why the fuck that nigga at my girl's house?" I asked, getting my shit together to leave.

I grabbed my other phone, sending out a text for the crew.

"Your crew is already ready, I tried calling you a few times, but couldn't get through. I got a hold of Diggy and E. You need to get to Lance; he's ready for takeoff."

I felt as if my soul was ripped from me. Volante or whatever the fuck his name was hated me for something I couldn't control. I just prayed he wouldn't harm Lo or Risa. One thing I wanted more than anything was to be able to kill that fuck-boy with my own hands.

LOVONNA

I have never been so afraid in my life. One minute I was on
the phone with Von, talking about moving in with him and
the next, I heard my friend screaming at the top of her lungs. I knew
Risa wasn't afraid of much. I was the one usually screaming from a
spider or some type of critter crawling around. I quickly got up from
my bed to see what was wrong with her. Once I made it into the living
room, I saw him. The same guy I thought that was Von in the grocery
store. He had a gun up to Risa's head. Once he saw me, he smiled and
then pushed Risa to the ground before snatching my phone. We all
heard Von yelling out my name. While the guy that looked like Von
talked to him, I thought about what my father told me before Risa and
I moved by ourselves.

*"LoVonna, you were eight years old when I first took you to the gun
range. After that, I took you every weekend. Why? Because I knew this day
would come for you to be on our own. That's why I got you this."*

*"You got me a gun?" I asked my father once he handed the rose gold
colored gun over to me. I took it and it looked so pretty.*

*"Do not let anyone know you have this, not even Risa. There may be a
day when you have to use it. I pray never, but I know this world is loaded
with sick, crazy, and confused people. You know the ends and outs of using*

163

this. Remember, if you have to use it, shoot to kill, baby girl. Don't let the enemy get another day to live. Call me, and I'll come and take care of the rest."

I took the gun with no thought about using it. I hugged my father, and he made me promise not to tell my mother as I promised him not to tell a lot of other shit.

Thinking back on the conversation my mom and I had about my father, I now knew what he meant by calling him to take care of the rest. But who he was now, didn't add up. Seeing that the guy was talking to Von, I had only a second to do what I needed to do. It was survival time and if the possibility of death was on the menu, I had to at least serve him with something he'd regret. I eased away as he told Von he was jealous of him. Risa was still on the floor. I think the girl was in shock. Once inside my room, I quickly walked into my closet and punched in the four numbers to my safe, grabbed my gun, and walked back into the living room.

"Where the fuck that bitch go?" he asked Risa. He was hovering over her while she sat on the floor. I cocked the gun, and he slowly turned around.

"I know you ain't going to do shit with that. You too damn fine to even have a gun in your possession. Now, I'm going to walk over to you and take it. I might let your fine ass live after doing some slick shit like that."

As he walked over to me, I quickly glanced at Risa. I stared at her and moved my eyes to the left, gesturing for her to move out the way because I was about to empty the clip. Once she did, I let off two shots that went straight to his head. He dropped before me, and I froze. I couldn't believe I had really shot him. It was us or him, and I damn sure didn't want it to be us.

"Oh my God, Vonna!" Risa yelled as she ran over to me. We hugged while I still held the gun.

"What are we going to do?" she asked.

"We? You didn't do or see nothing, Risa. Just leave, and I will call my dad or hell, even Von to take care of this. Just go."

164

"No, I'm not leaving you. I don't think anyone heard anything. What's on the tip of the gun?" she asked.

"A silencer."

"How do you even know how to use that thing?" she grilled.

"My dad taught me," I explained.

I snapped out of whatever trance I was in and quickly grabbed my phone from the guy. I FaceTimed Von, praying he would answer.

"Lil' baby, you good?"

"Yes," I said as a tear rolled down my left eye.

"Is he still there?" he asked in a calm voice.

"Yes."

"Where is he? Can he hear me?"

"He can no longer hear you."

"What? Lo, what the fuck is going on?" he mouthed.

I figured he thought that maybe I wasn't able to talk.

I mouthed back "He's dead."

"I'm fifteen minutes away, you sure?" he asked.

"I'm positive, just hurry, Von."

The tears came flowing down. Risa walked over to me and pulled me into a hug. I wasn't crying because of fear. I just felt things were about to reveal more than I bargained for.

"It's going to be okay; we're in this together," Risa said.

"What if I go to prison behind this?"

"Vonna, you won't. He was in our home with a gun. It's going to be okay."

Von announced that they were about to land, and he would be to me in a few seconds. I hung up, waiting for him to come. I quickly put the gun away.

After a few minutes, Von, E, Diggy, and six other guys came flying in. Von stopped at the body and stared down at it. He had one of the six men wrap the body up, while the others pulled out some type of solution and proceeded to clean the blood up.

"Come here, lil' baby," Von told me. I walked into his arm, and he held me tight.

"You okay?" he asked.

"Yes."

"Who killed him?" E asked.

Everyone looked around for an answer, and I didn't want to admit it, but I had no choice.

"I did," a deep voice spoke. I looked up and saw my father standing in the middle of my doorway. Although I felt safe in Von's arms, seeing my father gave me a great sense of security.

I watched as my father walked over to Von's crew and gave them tips on cleaning up the blood even though they were doing a good job. They didn't object; they listened and continued to do their job.

"Are you all okay?" my dad asked.

"Yes," Risa told him.

The men just kind of nodded.

Once the body was out, my dad asked to speak with me. I had so many questions, but I knew I couldn't ask in front of everyone. Once we got to the backyard, I started.

"Dad, what are you doing here?" I asked, as we both sat down.

"I came because I wanted to spend tomorrow with you. I wanted to talk because the last time I seen my princess she was running out of my house. I know I was wrong for what I said to you and also to LaVondrius. I'm a father, so I won't apologize for reacting the way I did. However, I shouldn't have said anything about his child to you. LoVonna, you're my world and all I want to do is see you happy. But before I get into all of that, what the fuck happened in there?" he whispered.

"I'm not sure, I don't even know how he found out where we lived."

"Do you think it was drug related?"

"Dad?"

"Vonna, I have the right to know. I did confess to a killing I know nothing about."

He got really close to me. Up close and personal.

"You know we can't talk about what's really going on, but don't get too caught up. I think you're in too deep," he told me.

"Mom told me about your past," I quickly changed the subject.

166

"I know, and I was so angry with her about that, but that's why I came to see you."

"Sir, can I talk with you two?" Von asked, walking up. Von stared between the two of us. I'm sure he noticed how close we were.

"LaVondrius, come sit," my dad said as he stood so that Von could sit. I looked between the two, wondering what would come next.

"Volante was my brother. I just found out that my dad had another son. I had people working on getting me information on him. When we took the cruise into the Bahamas, he was on it. Someone had to tell him that we were even going."

"You saw him on the boat? Wait, his name is Volante too?" I questioned.

"Yes, and yes. My father had him with another woman. My mother didn't want him in their lives, so my father didn't have anything to do with him."

"So, he's not your mother's child? All of this isn't making sense. Why didn't your father tell you he had another son?" I asked.

"I don't know. I'm working on finding that out."

It got quiet, so my father finally spoke.

"I was telling my daughter that I had no right to tell her about your son. I want to apologize for that. However, I am a father, and my daughter's best interest is my responsibility."

"Sir, I just want you to know that I'm not here to take advantage of your daughter. I care a lot about Lo. I know why you prejudged me, but it's more to me than what you think you know."

"I agree, young man. I came here to make amends with my daughter. I hate for my princess to feel like I'm trying to control her life to the point she won't even talk to me. I just ask that you give my daughter an opportunity to be all that she can be in life."

"I promise you, she's going to be," Von told him.

"Dad, I guess I better tell you now. I'm moving in with Von."

He was quiet at first, but I think he realized what was happening.

"So, you're doing your residency back home?"

"Yes."

"Good. Have you told your mother?"

167

"No, I will though."

"She'll be happy. She's very fond of LaVondrius."

"When did you kill him?" Von asked my father.

"You know the game, young man, never tell."

"I'm not staying here," I told them, changing the subject again.

"I figured. I got us a room across town. Sir, I'll put you in a room as well," Von stated.

"I'll be good here. Vonna go pack your things, and let me talk to him for a second."

I left to give them their privacy. I didn't know what else my father had to talk with him about. Once inside the house, I saw Risa getting her things together. We only had a week left of school. I was ready to go, I knew once I closed my eyes I would think about the body. I couldn't believe I killed someone although my father prepared me for it.

Inside our hotel room, I showered and then changed into my pajamas. Von had just came back from talking with his crew. I had been alone for about two hours. I talked to my mom and dad over the phone. I told her about me moving in with Von, and she had nothing bad to say. Her only wish was for me not to get pregnant. I promised her that I wouldn't.

"I brought you some food," Von said, walking into the room. He had us in the penthouse suite.

"Von, I'm afraid to go to sleep. I just killed someone. Should I be sad, scared, or even concerned?"

"I'm glad you finally confessed to it. I knew your father didn't kill him."

Damn, I fucked up. Oh, well, I have to talk with somebody about it. Should I just tell him? I'm going to blow it eventually anyway.

Von walked over to me and sat down. He pulled me onto his lap.

"Tell me what happened, and tell me what you wanted to talk to me face-to-face about."

I told him everything from the time we were talking up until I pulled the trigger.

"I don't know why he was there, Lo. I think he was going to use

168

you to get to me. It's so much shit I have to figure out, but I can't believe you killed him. You didn't tell me what you wanted to talk about."

"Von, I'm so scared. I'm so scared of losing everyone I've ever loved. Once I say this, I'm going to be viewed differently. I have to talk to Risa first before I tell you."

"It's that bad? What happened, lil' baby? Did you get raped?"

"Hell no!"

"How about we all get together and you tell Risa and I at the same time.'

"I guess but promise me one thing."

"What's that?" he asked.

"That you'll never question my love for you. Know that I love everything about you."

"I don't know what to say. You don't want to tell me now, so I guess I'll keep that thought in the back of my mind when you do decide to tell me."

After making love, Von held me until he thought I was asleep. He rolled over, and I waited patiently until he fell asleep himself.

It was late into night when I decided to leave and meet with my father. He said he needed to talk with me, but I needed to talk with him. I was tired of everything. Somethings just weren't worth it. I made sure I put it on Trigga good so that he wouldn't wake up. I hated I didn't bring my car because I would have to take his.

Pulling up to the location my father told me to meet him, I killed the engine and jumped out. It was really dark, but that didn't really bother me. Once inside of the building, I got on the elevator to the twelfth floor. From the outside, one would think that the place was somewhat abandoned, but the inside was very nice. I pressed the code into the keypad on the wall. The elevator took me right to the place where I was meeting my father. When the door opened, I got off and walked into the condo.

"I see you're driving that drug dealer's car," my father announced.

"I'm out," I told him.

"You have a job. So far, you're doing okay but you aren't doing enough. We should have this thing wrapped up. I thought by bringing his brother in it would make you do your fucking job."

"You brought his brother in? Why? I killed him because I thought he was there to hurt us."

"Oh, he was. That's why I came. I didn't know the amount of hatred he had for their father. I thought brining him in would help us, but hell, LaVondrius knew nothing of him. His brother doesn't know shit about their operation, so he had to die. I knew you'd kill him, so I set it up."

"What type of father are you?"

"One that will do anything to protect his family."

"How is this protecting me? I don't know who this OG person is, but whatever he wants, you might as well give it to him."

"I can't because what he wants, I no longer have. So, I promised him something else, I just need you to wrap shit up. Don't tell me you're really in love?"

"I told you I didn't want to be a part of this. I'm telling mom because this is too much for a twenty-year-old. I should be focusing on school."

"And another thing, are you really doing this physician bullshit?"

"I only came here to tell you that I'm out. If you want him, you'll have to figure another way out."

"You know who you're up against. Your mother and I won't be able to save you."

"I'll take my losses how they come. Don't forget, you have a past as well. I did my homework. OG wants your old empire, the one you promised him he could have. Only you gave it to the corner boy, who doesn't want to give it back. Now you're promising OG Trigga's empire. Only thing you forgot to mention was that his empire is passed down from his father. Even if Trigga isn't in the picture, OG still won't get it."

"Why the fuck you didn't mention that shit before."

"I tried telling you everything, but you kept drilling information in my head. I was naïve in the beginning, but I see now. Father, I love you to death, but I'm out of this. Yes, I do love LaVondrius."

"Once he knows what you were up to, he's not going to keep you in his life. You better hope he doesn't try to kill you. LoVonna, he is dangerous. Once you say those three letters, he's going to kill you without a doubt."

"He won't, because I haven't given' up any information. Everything I told you has been good. All this time you thought I was getting close to him to help you, but I was helping myself. I knew the first night I spent with him that I wasn't going through with it."

"What do you mean the first night?"

"When he first got out... look I have to go. He's going to wake up and wonder where I am."

"You better think long and hard about what you're going to do."

"My mind is made up. You on the other hand better figure something out. Why can't you just kill OG? Do he scare you that much?"

"No man scares me. I can't kill someone when I don't know where they're laying their head. Every time he calls me, he gives me a location to meet him. The calls are always private. I have no way to get to him."

"I have to go."

Something didn't feel right, so I got out of there. Once I got in my car, I looked at my phone. I had forty missed calls that fast. Trigga, Risa, and Diggy all called back to back. I knew it was now or never.

Walking into our suite, the crew was there staring at me if I was crazy. Risa ran over to me and hugged me with tears in her.

"I thought something happened to you," she cried.

"I just needed to get some air."

"Some air?" Von asked.

"Yeah."

"You went all the way over by Chesterfield Square, to get some air? The roughest part of LA. So, tell me why a girl like you would take her ass all the way over there?" Von asked.

The look he gave me let me know he wasn't falling for shit I had to feed him.

I closed my eyes and took deep breath. It was time I came clean.

"I guess now would be the right time to tell you all."

"Floor is yours, lil' baby," Von said.

I told them to all have a seat. I stood because I didn't know if sitting across from them would be a smart idea. Seeing all three pairs of eyes focused on me made me rethink, but I had to.

"Everything you guys know about me is true. There is only one thing that I have been lying about. Risa, do you remember the first time we met Diggy at the store, and your cousin introduced us to him?"

"Yeah, and when she told me he wanted to talk to me, I laughed, but you kept talking about him and pressured me to just talk to him. That night at the club, we hit it off and been kicking it ever since, but what does that have to do with you disappearing?" she asked.

"I did pressure you into talking to him. I needed you to. I needed to get into their circle to see how they operate, then Von came home. I was still going to do the job I was assigned to do, but seeing him for the first time at the club changed all of that."

"Fuck you mean a job?" Von asked me.

He stood up, and I was ready to run if need be.

"I was working undercover. My job—"

I didn't finish because Von was headed toward me. I ran around the other side of the couch as if it was going to stop him from getting to me.

"I know like hell you didn't say undercover? You a fucking snitch?" he asked.

"Let her finish because I know like hell this story better end well, or else," Diggy stated. He cocked his gun and pointed it toward me.

"Darcel, what are you doing?" Risa asked.

"Did you fucking hear what the fuck she just said?"

"Finish before I finish you," Von requested.

"My job was to tell the FBI all about your empire and how you operate. My father used to be in the game back in the day. He promised some guy who they call OG his empire. Only my father gave it to someone else. My father heard about your empire, but only he had to wait until you got out of prison, Von. I was supposed to get close to you and set you up. Once the FBI came in, OG was going to come in and rebuild what you had. Only they didn't know much about you. Being that you never told me about what you do in details, I didn't have anything to tell them. My father did some research and found out that you had a brother. He thought by paying him, that he would tell my father how you operate, only your brother had a great amount of hatred toward you. Nivea was brought in to get at Diggy because they knew Risa wouldn't turn on him, so they thought bringing in a beautiful girl would distract him."

"LoVonna, you knew who that bitch was? You would do that to me?" Risa asked.

"I knew Diggy wouldn't do that to you, so I didn't worry about her. I'm so sorry, you guys. Von, I never gave up any information on you. The day I first met you in the club, I knew I wanted you."

"Wait a minute… so what the fuck was that shit with Volante Jr.? Did you really kill him?"

"Yeah, I seen her do it," Risa spoke.

"I didn't know who he was until my father told me. My father set that up because he knew that I would kill him."

"This shit is fucking crazy, and I'm supposed to believe that you're clean. Why tell me this shit now?"

"Because I'm tired. I didn't want to do it, but this whole time I been pretending for my father. I led him to believe I was still working on the case."

LAVONDRIUS

"You know we have to kill this bitch, right?" Diggy stated.

"No!" Risa yelled.

"How can you still trust her after what she did?" he asked Risa.

"Because I've known her since elementary. I know it was fucked up, and I owe her an ass whooping, but I'm not letting you all kill her."

"So, what now?" I asked.

I didn't know what to say or do. I was in love with this girl, and she was working on cuffing a nigga for life. Fucking with the FBI, I would be in prison for the rest of my life. I wanted to off her, but I couldn't in front of Risa. Part of me wanted to forgive her, but I couldn't.

"I went to meet with my father. I told him I was out and now he's saying that they will take me down with you. I don't know how because I haven't said anything about what you do. As far as they know, you have legal businesses."

"This OG guy, where does he live?" I asked her.

"I don't know. My father doesn't even know."

She sat and told us all about her father, from what her mother told her. I understood he felt he had to try to take what is mine to get himself out of some shit, but the fucking FEDs? That's a whole different ball game.

"You want me to believe that things are just fine? All this time you been lying about who the fuck you really are. I'm lying next to the fucking FEDs in my fucking bed. How does that fucking look?"

"I'm not the FEDs," Lo stated.

"Oh, you're not? You fooled me, but then again, you're good at that shit, right? You're just a cover-up. But no matter how the fuck you look at the shit, you're still considered one of them," he voiced me.

"Can we talk in private?" she had the nerve to asked.

"Hell nah, because I'm out. I'm not about to sit in the room and hear shit else this bitch spitting. If we're not offing her, ain't shit to talk about," Diggy stated.

A part of me wanted to defend Lo, but then again, I felt where Diggy was coming from. He walked off, pulling Risa with him. She was fighting to get away, but Lo told her to just go. It was now her and I.

"Von, listen. My feelings for you are real."

"That's why you wanted me to keep that thought in the back of my mind. You really tried to cuff a nigga?"

"Do you believe me?"

"No."

"Von, I swear. I never gave up any information on you. Have I ever asked about what you do in the streets?"

"You know enough."

"Please, I know it was fucked up. But you have to believe me. I love you."

"I feel like all this shit is one big lie. I took your virginity, so part of me is wondering if you're telling the truth."

"I told you when I saw you in the club that I had already made up mind that I wasn't going to go through with it. I know you probably don't want to be with me, Von, and I understand that. But all I ask is that you forgive me."

"As much as I want to, Lo, I can't. You already put the bug in their ears."

"I didn't do shit, they had brought me in after everything was set-up. And still now, they have nothing on you."

"How do I know that, are you really a college student? How the hell you have all this time to do this shit?"

"Yes, I'm a college student. Everything you know about me is true. Our first night, that was real. Our first kiss, that was real. When I said I love you, that was real."

"If all that was real, why you didn't tell me that shit sooner?"

"The time frame doesn't matter. I love you, Von."

"Whatever we had is over, Lo. I got my crew here, which Diggy probably already put them up on game. So, you better be careful. I'm not going to make it my business to tell them not to harm you."

She looked to the ground, and it took everything in me not to run over to her. I had already sent a message out there while she was talking. My phone was in my hands the whole time. I told the crew she was off limits, if anyone was going to do anything, it would be me.

I gathered my things up and watched Lo closely. I noticed the tears she kept trying to wipe away.

"I'm out. You know it would had been better if you would had never told me that shit. But I guess I owe you something for coming clean."

"You don't owe me anything. The one thing I want, I know I won't ever get."

"What?" I asked curiously.

"Your heart."

"Yeah, you won't ever get that after that shit."

I walked away and out of the penthouse. I felt like I left my heart in the room with her. I never cried before, so the tear trying to form in my eye, I prevented it. I met up with the crew. Risa had gone up to check on Lo. No matter what, she was standing behind her friend.

"You think Risa in on the shit too?" one of our crew members asked.

"Nigga, do you get paid to ask questions?" Diggy asked him.

I chuckled because I knew that was coming.

"Risa said she's good until I come back. What you want us to do about Vonna's pops?"

"Leave him be for now," I told him.

I thought about how easy it was for Lo's father to look me in the eye and tell me all the bullshit he was saying.

"Lance about to land, so we about to be out," Diggy told me. I thought long and hard and knew it was best leaving shit where it was at.

~

It was early morning, and I was walking into my parents' house. My father sat at the table while my mother stood over the stove.

"Hey, son," my father spoke.

"Why the fuck you didn't tell me I had an older brother?"

His eyes got big as hell. My mother stood frozen with her mouth wide open.

"What are you talking about?" he asked.

"Don't fucking play like you don't know what I'm talking about? Volante Jr... your son!"

"Where did you hear that from?" Mom asked.

"From him."

"I didn't tell you because he's not my son. Yes, I fucked his mother, and she got pregnant, but he's not like us. I tried to build a bond with him, but he always pushed me away. He recently found out about you and reached out to me only to tell me that he hates me."

"Well, he's dead now."

"Dead?" he asked.

"Yes, I killed him," I lied.

"I can only imagine what went down. Son, it wasn't that I didn't want to tell you. Your mother wanted nothing to do with him."

"So, you abandoned your child because you couldn't keep your dick in your fucking pants? Are there any other children out there you want to tell me about?"

He started choking, and I stared into his eyes. I struck a nerve saying that. I saw his whole body language change.

"I wanted to make my wife happy. I fucked up and didn't know how to fix it. I guess I don't have to worry about fixing it now. I'm not going to ask why you killed him, because I know you as my son had a reason behind it."

I hugged my mom even though I wanted to be mad at her. She could have told me my father had another child. And to think my son was named after his ass. I chatted with my father, just to get a feel on a few things and then left.

"Hello?" Saver answered.

I called him because I needed him.

"Find Nivea."

"You got it."

I called the crew up because we had work to do. A nigga was tired, but I had to make sure everything was straight.

LARISA

I watched Vonna as she slept on the couch. She cried her eyes out all throughout the morning. Darcel and I got into a heated argument about me being around her, but I wasn't going to fuck over Vonna like that. I was still pissed, but I know she did what she thought she had too. Hell, when my father told me if I stopped seeing Darcel, he would leave him be, I did that shit. We were naïve to that street life.

Vonna was bathing when I walked into the bathroom.

"You okay?" I asked.

"How can you be concerned about me with what I did?"

"You're my best friend. I know why you did it. Yes, I'm still mad at you, but I love you more. So, yes, I'm concerned."

"I wish Von was so forgiving."

"That I can't help with, but I do know that he had given strict orders for no one to touch you."

"Really?"

"Yep, I was sitting next to him when Trigga called."

"I'm so sorry, Risa."

"We all make mistakes. I'm just glad you realized it before you got in too deep."

"Guess I'll be looking for a condo."

"Maybe, but probably not for long. However, I do find it quite strange that Trigga's son Volante, is named after his brother and father."

"I keep thinking the same thing, that's why I got a sample."

"A sample of what?" I asked.

"Blood and his hair to take to Jessica."

"Who's blood and hair?"

"Volante, Von's brother. I know the DNA results read that Von is the father, but I don't believe that shit. Either his father is the boy's dad, or his brother is."

"If that's the case, Layla been fucking the both of them, and they somehow tampered with the results."

"We will see. Thanks for sticking by my side."

"You're my best friend. I love you."

It was moving day. Darcel had the movers pack all my things. He even had them help Vonna with her stuff. Once they had everything packed, they drove those three hours to his place. Over the last few days, Darcel apologized for being hard on Vonna. We had decided that the movers will drive the truck, while he drove my car back. Vonna wanted to wait around for the results, so we stayed in the penthouse a bit longer because we weren't going to stay in a place where someone died. We didn't care who killed him.

"Thanks for staying behind with me," she stated.

"No problem. Is Jessica still stopping by today for drinks with us?"

"Yeah. She said she wanted to spend time with me before I left for good."

I had just washed, flat ironed, and installed bundles into Vonna's hair. I was curling it when there was a knock at the door. Vonna opened it, and it was Jessica. We had wine and vodka, but we all decided on the vodka.

"So, I wanted to tell you about the new girl that I was training. Her name is Nivea. This bitch wrote the result up to make it seem like LaVondrius was the father of four-year-old Volante Jr."

When she said that, we stopped what we were doing and paid full attention.

"So, he's not Von's?" Vonna asked.

"No, the DNA sample you got me was a match. He is Volante's Jr.'s dad. Which is so crazy because they're both juniors. But yeah, like I was saying. The executive heard some rumors and started to look into it. So, Nivea transferred here. Which is also crazy because if they find out she did some fraud shit, that bitch is done for good."

"What days do you work with her?" Vonna asked.

"Girl, every day, except Saturdays. You know I work Saturdays alone."

That was all the info we needed. I knew what Vonna was up to. I just hope Von believed her after all the shit that went down before. Nivea was playing with fire, and I was sure going to make sure her ass got burnt.

LOVONNA

I was laying in my old bed in my parents' house. My father was out of town, and I was happy about it. Although he never discussed anything around my mother, I still felt we left on bad terms. I was waiting on the perfect opportunity to reach out to Von to tell him about the results. To tell him that his son was really his nephew. I had Risa make a call for me, and I was waiting for her to call me back.

I was about to go for a ride when Risa called.

"Hello?"

"Hey, girl, so, I called Truth, like you asked me. She agreed to meet with you. She also wanted to know why the hell you didn't call your damn self."

"Does she not know?" I asked Risa.

"I don't think so, and she didn't act as if she knew."

"Interesting. So I have to live that nightmare over again?"

"I believe so, but call her, she's waiting on your call."

After hanging up, I called Truth. We spent hours talking on the phone. Come to find out, Von told her everything. But she didn't say much over the phone. She just said she knows he still loves me and that I still have a chance to cuff him. We made a joke of it, although it wasn't funny because Von stated I was trying to cuff him for life, meaning send him away to prison for good. We setup a time to meet. I had a few hours, so instead of going for a ride, I decided to just chill. I got on Facebook and noticed that Musiq had sent a message.

Musiq: *Vonna, I still love and miss you. I wish things could have went differently.*

Me: *Musiq, it's been years, and things ended just like they should have.*

Musiq: *I wanted to tell you that I'm attending college now. Football didn't work out like I wanted it to, but hey at least I'll have a degree. My father said I could come work with him once I'm done.*

I thought that was great. Musiq's father was a businessman. He worked so much that he was absent for most of Musiq's life.

Me: *That's great. But I really think we shouldn't communicate at all. It's just best that way.*

I waited but got no response back. I could clearly see that he read the message. I guess he didn't like what I said to him. I just didn't want to lead him on by thinking we could communicate in anyway. There's a reason why you leave people in your past.

Walking in the park with Truth and Baby was nice. There was actually a nice breeze coming through. I told her everything, and she had yet to say anything about it.

"So, why didn't you go through with the plan?" she asked.

"The person they portrayed him to be wasn't the person I saw walking into the club that night. I saw a man who needed someone he could trust. A man who needed real love. Everything about him seems flawless. Even when he mentioned what he did, I still didn't judge him. I know the struggle of a black man. It's hard to succeed when you have a lot against you, but he's accomplished so much. I don't see potential, I see success, ambition, and dedication. He has no fears, but yet he fears God. I don't know why my father thinks by him being out the way, we will even his debt with this OG guy. Everything I said to LaVondrius is true. I love him; I'm in love with him. I know he won't forgive me. I wouldn't forgive if it was the other way around."

"But you said the day he walked into the club, you knew you

weren't going to go through with it. So, if you didn't go against him, there was no harm done."

"Yes, but I knew they were out to get him and I didn't say anything. I was so naïve and just gullible. I pressured Risa into talking to Diggy, which I knew once she got in good with him, I could get more info on their operations, but I just couldn't bring myself to go through with it. The Nivea chick, which turns out she knows Layla very well. Which is crazy because she was also working together with Volante Jr., the oldest. I know I should tell Von first, but I have to tell you."

"Tell me what? There's more?"

"Yes, so they brought Nivea in to see if she could get close to Diggy. But we didn't know that she was also cool with Layla. Apparently, Layla and Volante Sr. paid Nivea to change the results of the DNA test. Volante is not Von's son. It's his nephew."

"Nephew? So, the Volante guy, who was Trigga's brother, is Volante's Jr.'s father?"

"Yes, but what I found out from my girl, Jessica, is that Volante Sr. thought the child was his, he didn't want his son to know that he was having sex with his ex-girlfriend."

"Wait. You mean to tell me that bitch was fucking the father and both brothers? Wow! I think you need to tell Trigga this now."

"He's not going to want to talk to me."

"He will. Give me an hour, and he'll be calling you to come by the house."

"I doubt that, but thanks for listening and not judging me. I know it was wrong, I don't know what will happen, but I feel things are about to fall apart."

"They won't. All you need to worry about is getting your man back, and I'm going to help you."

I carried Baby back to the car and watched them drive off. The sun was going down, so I decided to just go back to my parents' house. I found a condo that wasn't too far from Risa and Diggy that was a reasonably priced, but I was holding off on buying it for some reason.

Hours had gone by, and I didn't hear anything from Truth. I

figured Von didn't want anything else to do with me, and I had come to terms with that.

"I thought you were sleep," my mom said, walking in.

"No, just laying here. Where are you going?" I asked her.

"Vonna, I told you earlier today that I was going to Cleveland. I may be partnering with this attorney who is well respected for his work. He is moving here, so we're trying to get him into our firm. I know you don't like hearing about that boring stuff."

"No, I think that is great. I wish you luck. Are you driving?"

"Girl, no. I'm flying. The driver should be pulling up soon. I just came to say 'I love you'."

"I love you too, Mom."

"What's going on with you?"

"Nothing, I'm good."

"LaVondrius?"

"Yeah, I think it's over between us."

"Really? Well only time will tell. I have to get going. I'll lock up, so don't worry about getting up."

She kissed my cheek and left. I wished I had more time to talk with her, but I knew she had to get going. I ran my bath water and came back out into my room to get my things together after I bather. When I heard my doorknob turn and I don't know why, but I thought about OG. What if he was coming to kill me for not going through with the plan?

When the door opened, my heart stopped. I didn't know if running was an option because I only had one other place to run and that was the bathroom.

"You fixed your mouth to tell me about how you were, or if you still working undercover, but couldn't tell me that Volante isn't my son?" Von asked.

"I'm not working undercover. My father is handling whatever business he has to because he knows I'm out. Von, I'm so sorry. I wish I could take it all back. I was going to tell you about the DNA test, but I didn't think you would even talk to me. And how did you get in here?"

"Your mother before she came to tell you she was leaving."

"I don't know what to say, Von. I know you don't trust me, but how I feel about you is real."

"How you feel about me? You really expect me to believe that shit? Y'all bitches ain't shit. Look at Layla, she fucked me, my brother, and my pops. How the fuck does that even sound? And you… I did my research as well. Everything you said was true, up until you said you really loved me. I know about your father's past, and the shit he was into. Your mother told you a lot, but she didn't tell you enough. Your father used to run with my father back in the day. The OG person your father told you about is my father. That's why my father hated you so much, I knew it was something because you seemed perfect, and I knew he didn't really want me to be with Layla. He just didn't want me to be with the daughter of the one person who he envied. Your father had a nice operation going, one that is still out-doing mine 'til this day. My father thought that by taking over your father's empire, it would give him this power over your father. Then your father had already given it to his son. Yes, LoVonna, I'm not the only one who has or should I say, had a brother. Your father has another woman, and she lives in Cleveland. Your mother wasn't lying about doing business there, but she failed to tell you she's going to catch your father in a lie. The corner boy your father told you he sold his empire to is his very own son."

He's lying, he just wants to hurt me. My father wouldn't cheat on my mother.

Tears rolled down my face, and the evil look Von had plastered on his face had vanished. He looked at me for a brief second and turned to walk away.

"So, that's why you came here? To hurt me?"

He turned around and walked over to me. I looked up into his eyes, and I just needed for him to pull me into his arms. To tell me that he forgave me and that he made all of that shit up. But, he didn't, instead he smiled.

"Checkmate, don't ever contact Truth again. You come around again, and I will kill you myself. Detective LoVonna."

"I'm not a detective."

He smirked and walked away. I felt as if I was dreaming. I got up and rushed down the stairs. Von was pulling off when I made it to the window. I locked the door when my home phone started ringing, so I answered right away.

"Hello?"

"Vonna, I been trying to get in touch with you for hours. Why is your phone off?" Risa asked.

"My phone isn't off."

"Not off as in the power, like disconnected."

I ran upstairs to see, and sure enough it was.

"I was trying to see what was going on. I overheard Darcel tell E about your father, and Von's father. It's so much shit going on."

"I know, I think I should go to a hotel for the night. For some reason, I don't feel safe here."

"I think you should too, also do something to get your phone back on. Do you need money?"

"Girl, no. I'll call you when I make it to the room from the hotel phone."

"Okay, and Vonna, please be safe."

I was inside of my room packing my things when my room door came open. I thought it was Von, but I remembered I locked the door. I quickly turned around and it was Volante Sr.

"Nice home, I see you ran my son away. I thought I would be hiding in the closet for a while."

"What do you want?"

"Is that any kind of way to talk to your father-in-law?'

"Father in-law? You don't even like me."

"It's not that I don't like you, it's your father who I don't like. He promised me his empire, but he had given that shit away and now he refuses to turn it over. Then he told me about someone else's empire that I could easily take over. He just needed to make them disappear forever. That's where you came in at. When I learned it was my own son, I thought, 'what a blessing it would be for him to be put away forever'. I could raise my son in peace."

"Your son, I'm sorry to tell you, but Volante isn't yours. You were so busy trying to make the results show that Von was the father that you didn't even see the actual results."

"What the hell are you talking about?"

"I know all about what you and Layla did, and it doesn't make since because if you wanted Von out of the picture. Why go through so much to make him think he had a son? Or was it that you didn't want him to know you were fucking his ex."

"Since you're not going to go through with the plan, you might as well die. You know too much and that makes you a liability."

"I would say it makes her an asset."

Volante Sr. and I both looked behind him and it was his wife. Tanah stood there with a gun in her hand that was pointed at her husband. Von was standing right behind her.

LAVONDRIUS

*W*hen I left Lo's house I went straight to my pops crib. I had a bone to pick with him, but he wasn't there. My mom was on her way out, and I asked where she was headed. When she told me, I wondered why? It wasn't everyday your mom would leave late night to go over to your girl's house. She told me she thought my father was creeping with Vonna. I laughed because I knew that would never happen. But to ease her mind, I rode with her. When we got there and up the stairs, we heard everything as we stood in the doorway of Lo's room. My heart dropped because everything Lo said was true. My father was a real snake, and how he played my mother was fucked up.

"Tanah, baby, what are you doing here?"

"I think I should be asking you that."

"It's not what you think. This girl has been—"

"Stop it. Don't fix your mouth to tell another lie. I will not accept it this time. So, Volante Jr. is really yours? You would stoop that low and sleep behind your son and have a baby with his ex? All while having a wife at home? I wish Joseph would have killed you back in the day."

"Fuck him, if he wouldn't have been with Tasha, your dick hopping ass would have been with him. You don't think I know about your crush on him!" my pops yelled at her.

"Out of all places in the state of California that you could be, you choose to be in my home. Which makes it liable for me to kill you," Lo's father said. I don't know if she was happy or mad to see him.

"I was never hiding from you, if you really wanted me, you would have found me," my pops stated.

"Vonna, go downstairs, get into your car and drive to wherever Risa is at. I will call you when you can return," Joseph told her.

She didn't hesitate to leave. I wanted to follow her, but I needed to stay.

"You're going to kill me in front of my son and wife?" my dad asked.

I had to chuckle at that one my damn self.

"You can't be serious," I said, walking toward him. When I got closer, he pulled his gun out of his back pocket.

"Still, you don't get it. Haven't I taught you anything? Never walk up on your enemy without defending yourself," my dad stated. He pointed his gun at me.

"Our son shouldn't have to defend himself against his own father," my mother spoke.

She let off three shots into his chest, and not one time did I feel pain for him. He fell to the ground, gasping for air. Another shot was let off by Joseph, who shot my pops in the head while he was lying on the ground.

My mom ran over to me and held me tight. I kept my eyes on Joseph.

"LaVondrius, I am deeply sorry about what was plotted against you. Had I known your father's whereabouts, I would had killed him a while ago. OG is a snake, as you already know. It was his idea to get Saliburry involved. He had him pretend like he was the FEDs to make LoVonna believe that we really had something on you. A father should protect his daughter, and that's what I thought I was doing. If OG, your father knew she really cared for you, he would have probably killed her. I knew about your brother, and I always wondered why

OG wasn't taking care of him. So, when I ran into Volante Jr., I asked why he was in town. He said he came to get his son. But I found out through the grapevine that he had other motives and that was to take you and your father out. So, I started working with him to find your father. I only told LoVonna half the truth about him. Now Nivea, she and Volante Jr. met while visiting Layla. He asked Layla about his son, and she told him what she did with the DNA results. So, after that, Nivea agreed to help Volante Jr. after he threatened to kill her for changing the results to say you were Volante's father. Your father really thought he was that boy's dad. I know all of this is a lot, and I hate that I pulled my daughter in to make her believe she was really working under-cover."

"You got someone to clean this up, I'm assuming?" I asked him, ignoring what he just stated.

"Yes, now I'd advise you two to get out of here. I see you have no interest of hearing what I got to say, and I understand that."

I walked my mom out, and I helped her into the car. I pulled off, heading to my home. I knew she needed to be around me for a few days. Once I got in, Truth was there, and she quickly helped me get my mother into one of the guest rooms. My mom was quiet and help-less. She wouldn't move, talk, or anything.

"What happened?" Truth asked once she got into the living room. I told her everything, and she just shook her head. I was still unclear on somethings, but I wasn't in my right mind to figure it out. My own father wanted me out the way, so he could basically raise his child that he led me to believe was mine. I was trying to rack my brain to make everything make sense, but in reality, my father wasn't never really a father. He never wanted me to go legit, but he wanted his empire back. His motive was still unclear. Lo had her story and Joseph had his. I'm sure my mother had her own to tell, but I was tired of hearing it all.

"LaVondrius, just go get her. You know you love her, so just go find her and tell her how you feel."

"I fucked up and did some spiteful shit. I told her this lie about her father having another child and her mother going to Cleveland to find her husband because she knows he's cheating. Just a bunch of shit I made up."

"I know like hell you didn't do that! Why?"

"I wanted to kill her so bad, but I love her too much. So, I had to hurt her some type of way. I couldn't believe she even believed half the shit I told her."

"So, what? Are you going to go get your woman?"

I made sure my mom was good, showered, and then headed to Diggy's crib. When I got there, everyone was there too, including Neen and E. All eyes were on me, walking into the house, and Master jumped on my leg. Usually, I would play with him, but I wasn't in the mood.

"Another time, Master," I told him. He ran away and Lo turned around, looking at me. Her back was faced toward me, so she never saw me come in.

"Let me holla at you?" I told her.

The eyes that were on me were now on her.

"Why?"

I gave her a look to not fuck with me. I had come in peace, but she was already fucking up. I guess E saw my expression because he excused himself along with everyone else. When the room was clear, I made my way over to Lo.

"I'm sorry," I told her.

"You're sorry? Is this some joke?" she asked. I looked at her appearance, and she looked drained. I knew the stress level that was on her, but she brought most of it on herself.

"I'm sorry because I lied about your father. He isn't cheating on your mother nor does he have a son."

"What? Why would you lie? I sat here telling everyone what I was going to say and do when my father called me. Why would you make that up, Trigga?"

I smirked at her calling me Trigga.

"Because I was pissed at you. But on the real, all that shit don't make sense. All I got from it was that my father hated me so much, he was willing to do anything to hurt me. I do want you to know that I am still mad at you being that your father told me you weren't undercover for the FEDs, only Saliburry. Saliburry had some explaining to do on his part, but I know my father probably compensated him good for his services."

"What you mean, I wasn't really undercover?"

"All that don't even matter, Lo. I'm here because I love you, lil' baby. I keep telling you that you cuffed a nigga. I just want to know the honest truth."

"What truth?" she asked.

"You thought you were really undercover, so tell me this. Everything we experience together, the love you say you have for me, is it real?" I questioned.

"From the day I met you in the club, I knew I wanted you. Remember our night together? All of that was real. Von, I can't fake those type of feelings. I love you so much."

She started crying, and I knew she was telling the truth. I don't know why we had so many odds against us, but I finally figured we had it right.

"You still moving in with a nigga?"

"If you still want me."

"I wouldn't be asking. We have a lot to talk about, including what I'm going to do with Volante."

"What you mean?"

"His mother is dead?"

"Wait, what? How? When?"

"I told you, when Trigga feels crossed, Trigga X's them out."

"Where is Volante?" she questioned.

"At the house with Truth now. I had my peeps pick him up and handle her."

"Not in front of him, I hope?"

"What I look like? I wouldn't do no shit like that."

"I'm sorry, Von, do you forgive me?"

"I do, but don't ever pull no snitch shit like that. We kill niggas for shit like that. I know you wanted to cuff a nigga, but damn."

"Stop it, I think we need to just take it slow. Start over and build together."

"We can build, but taking it slow, fuck all of that. We in deep already. I need you, lil' baby. I ain't never needed a woman for shit, but you, I need all of you."

She stood face to face with me and wrapped her arms around my neck. I loved when she did that shit. We kissed and heard some commotion behind us.

"Man, I'm glad that shit is over. I thought we was really gon' have to murk sis," Diggy said, laughing.

"I don't find that funny one bit," Lo told him.

After clearing up a few things with them and talking one-on-one with Diggy and E about what we wanted to do with Nivea, Lo and I finally left to go home. Her father called her while I was driving. He wanted to meet up the next day to discuss somethings.

Inside of my bedroom, Vonna and I were cuddled up just talking when a knock was heard on my door. I told whoever it was to come in.

"Hey, don't mean to disturb you two, but I just need to get something off my chest," my mother said.

Lo and I raised up, giving my mother our undivided attention.

"I know I haven't been the best mother to you, Trigga. Let me stop calling you that, I didn't name you Trigga. I name you LaVondrius. I was so busy trying to be the best wife, I neglected my duties as a mother. I thank God Truth was here to lead you on the right path. Son, you are my world, and I love you more than anything. I want to take Volante. You don't deserve that responsibility and neither does this beautiful girl here. He can stay with me once I move. I can't live in that home that I shared with your father. Volante will give me the chance to be the mother I always wanted to be. Every time I tried to do things a certain way with you, your father would say I was being too easy on you and that I shouldn't be babying or nurturing you, because you would grow up to be soft. The only thing that did was prevent me from being the mother I should have been. I'm so sorry that after all these years, I didn't do right by you."

I tried like hell to hide the tears that came from my eyes, but I couldn't. She just didn't know how good it felt for her to say those words to me. All I ever wanted was for my mother to be a mother to me. I see that my father really fucked up our family as a whole with his wicked ways. I was glad that he was dead.

"Thank you, Mom, and it's no problem for me to still take care of Volante."

"No, live your life and when it's time for you two to have children, I want you two experience that together. Not to be induced into it. Of course, I'll need you around to help make him a man, but that's what an uncle is for, right?"

We talked for hours when Truth came in to join us. Volante was sleep in his room, and if I could, I would have had everyone under one roof. But I knew Lo wasn't having that shit, and besides, I loved how she called out my name while I was hitting it from the back.

Five years later...

LAVONDRIUS

"What does the results say?" I asked the physician.

"You may need surgery LaVondrius, the pain you're feeling in your groin is from inguinal hernia pain. Surgery may not be necessary, so I'm going to refer you to a specialist."

"Why? You are special enough, with your sexy ass. You gettin' thick, lil' baby," I told Lo. My baby was practicing and doing her thing as a physician. I told her about the pain I was having, and she wouldn't let another day go by without me coming in to be seen. At first, I thought it was weird having my girl care for me, but she made me feel comfortable telling her my personal shit.

"Von, I told you to be professional when we are here."

"Why? Can't nobody hear us? Besides, I'm ready to bend you over on this table. You lookin' all sexy today. I know niggas be hittin' on you, don't they?"

"No, they don't."

"Yeah, right. You wouldn't tell me anyway."

"You're right, because I don't need you up here disturbing my patients."

"Whatever, but is you pregnant?"

"Why would you ask me that?"

"Because, I saw the home pregnancy test in the garbage at home. So, is you?"

"No, it was negative. Even the one I took a few days ago here was negative. I know you want a child, but maybe it isn't the right time."

"I know, but hell you're twenty-five years old."

"What that mean? I'm fine and in my prime still."

"Don't I know it, but we seen a specialist already. He said everything's working, so I mean, maybe we need to fuck more," I told her.

"Really? I work from 7:30 a.m. to 6:00 p.m. and we still manage to get it in three times a day? I don't think that's an issue. I mean, maybe it's too soon to tell. I have been feeling nauseous lately."

"We just have to wait and see, but in the meantime, let me bend you over real quick."

"Von, I have another patient I have to see like ten minutes ago. I'll see you at home. Is Volante still coming over tomorrow night?" she questioned.

"Yes."

Volante was nine years old and acted just like me. He knew I was his uncle, because as he got older we told him about his father and that he had died. My mother did take him in, but he spent almost every weekend at my house. We also told him about his mother dying, which really hurt him. It almost made me regretful for killing her dumb ass, but I got over it. He really loved Lo and enjoyed spending time with the both of us. She had his ass so damn spoiled. He called my mother, grandma and of course that lil' nigga loves his granny. She really showed that she was capable of being a great mother, and I loved her for that. She was seeing some guy that I have met only once. And for a square ass nigga, he really made her happy.

"Oh, I kind of told Neen that we will watch lil' E as well," Lo mentioned.

"Oh, hell nah. That lil' nigga eat too damn much. And your ass hate getting up early on the weekends, so I know when his greedy butt wakes up crying to eat early morning, I'll be the one to get up."

"Von, stop it, he's two now, and remember how he wasn't eating much and the doctors were so worried? Let's be thankful he's eating now."

"Yeah, eating the whole damn house."

"I'm telling E you be getting on his son."

"Tell him, shit he know. Him and Neen be waiting until his fat butt go to sleep before they eat their snacks. Now, who has to sneak and eat? Only a fat child's parent."

We laughed so hard, but I was only joking. I love lil' E's ass to death. He brought so much joy to my boy and Neen. I couldn't wait to feel that joy.

Once I left Lo to finish seeing her patients, I headed over Diggy's crib.

"Aye, bro, you know my girl told me that she wants to finally have a baby. Man, a nigga so happy. She stopped taking the shots now, so a nigga been shooting them up in her ass. I know she probably carrying twins," Diggy said.

"Man, your ass stupid. But, we been trying. I hope you have a girl, nigga."

"Why wish that karma on me?"

"We got Volante and lil' E. We need a girl in the family."

"Okay, let it be you. I'm having twin boys, fuck that. I'm not dealing with a lil' girl. A nigga like me will go to prison for life if I find out a lil' boy looking at her wrong."

"Man, you right, you don't need a girl."

"Shit, but once Risa get off, we'll be over there. You know I got that good shit."

"I already know. Lo talking about she want me to stop smoking because of this damn hernia. I told her ass that it don't hurt when I smoke."

"That's why you been complaining about not being able to perform your best in bed?"

"Nigga, I ain't never said no shit like that. I said the pain be slowing me down sometimes. Get out of here with that. I don't care if I'm having a stroke, I'm going to be all up in that pussy of mine."

"Pussy-whipped ass. Y'all came a long way though. Shit, hell, we all did."

"One thing I can honestly say is, it feel good to be legit."

"Man, I got another year, and I'll be saying the same. But you still be helping me out nigga, so your hand still in it."

"True, I can't let it go completely, but not making all the decision is like a fucking relief."

"Yeah, I hear that. So, you still gon' pop that question?" he asked me. I had mentioned to him and E that I was going to ask Lo for her hand in marriage. After talking with her parents and getting their blessing, I wanted to do it right before the ball drops the following week.

"I am, right before the ball drops."

"I'm going to ask Risa as well."

"You lying, for real nigga?"

"I'm serious. I talked with her father and he gave his blessing. You already know her momma excited about it, but on the low, I think her moms want some of this."

"Nigga, Latrell gon' kill your ass."

"I'm serious, she always talking about sex around me. I'm gon' bend her ass over and give her what she wants. Shit, Risa come from the pussy, and if her pussy good, I know the momma pussy gotta have a nigga doing the retard move."

I laughed so hard because his ass was out of his mind. We joked like that all the time. Never in front of the women though because we knew that they wouldn't have found that shit funny at all.

Everyone was in my home just relaxing. The guys and I were playing cards while Risa and Neen decided to join us. Neen was good at playing cards, but Risa was fucking up. She and Diggy started to argue about the game.

"Girl, do you know my mom wants to keep lil' E all week?" Neen asked Lo.

"So, he's not coming over?" Lo asked.

"Nope."

"Good. His greedy ass be wanting to eat from sun up to sun down," I added.

"First off, don't come at my son like that. And second, you be the main one asking for him to come over."

"Yeah, but not spend the night."

"Anyway, Vonna. We should all go out tomorrow since she's keeping him. We haven't turned up in a while."

"Yes, let's go. That dress the designer made me, I've been dying to wear."

"Oh, just wait until you see the one they made me for my birthday," Neen added.

"I hope they have my New Year's outfit on point," Lo told her.

After we all talked and chilled, everyone left. I pulled Lo onto my lap as we sat in the living room.

"You are so amazing, you know that?" I asked.

"I do now. Thank you for being my rock, Von."

"Always, baby, I told you it's me and you 'til the world blow."

"You know, sometimes the best way to do a pregnancy test is with a blood sample?"

"Oh, yeah?"

"Yep, I was going to wait until New Year's, but I'll tell you now. I did a blood sample today, and I'm pregnant—six weeks to be exact."

I turned her face toward me to see if she was serious.

"You for real?"

"I am."

"Damn, well you know I wanted to ask you something on New Year's Eve, but I guess I can ask you now."

"Okay, what?"

I pulled her from my lap and walked into my office to get the ring. When I returned, she was laid across the couch looking so beautiful.

"LoVonna, that day in the club I saw so many women I wanted to take home and fuck. But, you, I wanted more. I wanted something from you that I didn't even know about at the time. In the beginning, things were rocky but we found our balance. We found what works for us. I always say you cuffed a nigga. Now, I'm trying to cuff you. Lil' baby you cuffed a street king, but you made me a real man. I want to ask for your hand in marriage."

I got down on one knee as she stood to her feet. She started crying, and she was trying to talk, but I didn't understand one word she was saying.

"I don't understand, lil' baby."

She wiped her tears away and cleared her throat.

"I said, of course I want to cuff you for life. Yes, I will marry you."

We had so much to look forward to. A baby and a wedding. Also, Diggy and Risa's wedding because I knew he would be right behind us. Life was good for a nigga, and I never liked to compare myself to niggas, but one thing we all had in common was that we all got cuffed by our lil' babies.

THE END

A NOTE FROM THE AUTHOR

Thank you for reading this new series, *Lil' Baby Cuffed a Street King 2.* I hope you enjoyed your read. I want to thank you all for being supportive throughout this series. Stay tuned for *a hot new series* coming soon. **Please leave a review**. While you wait, I still have other great reads that you can check out. Also, check out my author page where I drop sneak peeks and much more. Keep rocking with your girl! Peace and love!

Author
T'Nesha Sims
Pen Sensation

ABOUT THE AUTHOR

T'Nesha Sims born in Los Angeles, California raised in Michigan where she lived majority of her life. Discovering her passion at an early age of 10, when she wrote short poems. T'Nesha attended Baker College where she obtained her Bachelors degree in Human Resource Management, and now works as a Human Resource Manager.

In 2013 T'Nesha wrote and finished her first manuscript and had no direction on where to go with it. With support and motivation from family and friends she decided to pursue her dreams and submitted her submission for review. In September 2016 she signed with Royalty Publishing House. She never thought that her dreams would become her reality. She's glad she never gave up on her passion for writing, because now she is living her dream.
STAY CONNECTED

Amazon: Author Tnesha Sims
Email: Author Tenesha Sims

Royalty Publishing House is now accepting manuscripts from aspiring or experienced urban romance authors!

WHAT MAY PLACE YOU ABOVE THE REST:

Heroes who are the ultimate book bae: strong-willed, maybe a little rough around the edges but willing to risk it all for the woman he loves.

Heroines who are the ultimate match: the girl next door type, not perfect - has her faults but is still a decent person. One who is willing to risk it all for the man she loves.

The rest is up to you! Just be creative, think out of the box, keep it sexy and intriguing!

If you'd like to join the Royal family, send us the first 15K words (60 pages) of your completed manuscript to submissions@royaltypublishinghouse.com

LIKE OUR PAGE!

Be sure to <u>LIKE</u> our Royalty Publishing House page on Facebook!

CPSIA information can be obtained
at www.ICGtesting.com
Printed in the USA
LVHW05s2030180618
581092LV00015B/1244/P